DR. ADRIANA EARTHLIGHT

STUDENT SHRINK

DR. ADRIANA EARTHLIGHT

STUDENT SHRINK

A NOVEL BY BONNIE ZINDEL

Viking Kestrel

For David and Lizabeth with love

VIKING KESTREL
Published by the Penguin Group
Viking Penguin Inc., 40 West 23rd Street, New York, New York 10010, U.S.A.
Penguin Books Ltd, 27 Wrights Lane, London W8 5TZ England
Penguin Books Australia Ltd, Ringwood, Victoria, Australia
Penguin Books Canada Ltd, 2801 John Street, Markham, Ontario, Canada L3R 1B4
Penguin Books (N.Z.) Ltd, 182–190 Wairau Road, Auckland 10, New Zealand

Penguin Books Ltd, Registered Offices: Harmondsworth, Middlesex, England

First published in 1988 by Viking Penguin Inc.
Published simultaneously in Canada

10 9 8 7 6 5 4 3 2 1
Copyright © Bonnie Zindel, 1988
All rights reserved

Library of Congress Cataloging in Publication Data
Zindel, Bonnie.   Dr. Adriana Earthlight, student shrink.
Summary: Adriana Earthlight, Jefferson High School's favorite self-trained shrink, falls in
love and decides to concentrate on her most important case—herself.
[1. High schools—Fiction. 2. Schools—Fiction. 3. Psychology—Fiction] I. Title.
PZ7.Z645Dr 1988   [Fic]   87-29835   ISBN 0-670-81647-7

Printed in the United States of America by Arcata Graphics, Fairfield, Pennsylvania
Set in Times Roman

DR. ADRIANA
EARTHLIGHT

STUDENT SHRINK

ONE

Folks will have a second chance of being millionaires in the largest Lotto jackpot in history. The only winning ticket was disqualified because it was purchased by a sixteen-year-old boy. Eighteen is the magic number, the radio blasted a few inches from my ear. A sixteen-year-old boy from the Bronx wasn't considered old enough to be lucky.

I turned my radio-alarm off. It was 6:40. My first case would be waiting for me at the deli in an hour and I couldn't be late. Not today. This was the first few hours on Eastern Standard Time, and I hoped Carolyn had remembered to turn back her clock. Spring forward, fall back. I wondered when my hour would be, the hour I could call my very own.

I jumped out of bed. The comforter had fallen to the floor. Tiny goose feathers in the pink and blue nosegay comforter had collected at the bottom. With a few hearty shakes, the goose down returned to its rightful place.

With no time to lose, I rushed to the bathroom, splashed my face with water, then pulled my hair into a French braid. When I looked up, Mom was in the doorway watching me. She was wearing those furry mukluks of hers, the kind the Indians wore when they sold Manhattan for the price of a really good Chinese dinner. Compared to my nervous energy, Mom, in her blue Art Deco robe, and matching blue, blue eyes, exuded a certain calm. Hopefully, one day, I might relax into that hormonal balance, but I didn't foresee that in the near future.

"Up early," Mom observed.

"Late. Meeting Carolyn at the deli."

Strands of loose hair fell back onto my face as I pulled on a large green jersey shirt and faded jeans.

"So here's breakfast to go." She offered me the usual—a grilled cheese English muffin.

"Ahhah." I took a few bites, then tossed the rest in the garbage.

"Student shrinks need a good breakfast, too. You're still growing."

"Mom, I'm sixteen. Please don't baby me anymore," I said. The other part was all right, the student shrink part. It was a description I latched onto when Kathy Lipkin wrote it across my face in last year's yearbook. Although the red ink made me look as if I was suffering from gingivitis, the inscription meant more to me than any flattering dedication could. But if the powers that be ever got their hands on this book, they'd be more than inviting me down to the headmaster's office. The guidance counselor, Mrs. Crumper, would have me building math credits in Siberia, and not as part of any student exchange program.

Mom poured herself her third cup of coffee. "Was that your phone ringing last night, or 7C?"

"Mine," I answered, staring out the window at the one solitary tree on our block. It was the only remnant of the old church that had been there before it was torn down to make room for a modern high rise. "Do you think my phone is directly over consecrated ground?" I asked.

"Probably. But at two in the morning?"

"Miranda couldn't sleep and Lauren was in a bad way."

"Again?"

"Lauren's father told her his magazine might be transferring him to Saudi Arabia this time. That would make her seventh move in eight years, Mom. She even writes her address in a number two pencil." I gulped down the rest of the Cranapple juice. "And, to make it worse, her parents had a fight. Her mother said she couldn't move anymore and her father . . ."

"Yes?"

"Sorry, Mom—" I caught myself. "Confidential."

"But I'm your mother. It doesn't count."

"My lips are sealed," I said, zipping them up.

"Miranda. Lauren. Carolyn. All the others. I just wish you didn't have everyone's problems on your mind." She followed me to the closet as I pulled out my denim jacket.

"Mom," I protested, zipping it up, "I can't help it. I've got to be there for them. Wouldn't you?"

"I just worry about you, that's all," she said, fixing my collar.

I tossed the red backpack over my shoulder and dashed out the door. "And I'm sorry about all those phone calls. I'll pay for them out of my allowance," I promised as I rang for the elevator.

"Forget it," Mom called after me. "You can't help it if you're working the night shift." She watched me pacing nervously, waiting for the elevator. "And be good at school today. I don't want that guidance counselor calling to say my daughter's driving her crazy down there. One more time and she can suspend you."

"Mom, she's got wax in her ears."

Mom held her hands over her ears like a rabbit, wiggling her fingers. She did have a way with words.

Fortunately, the elevator made an express trip and I dashed

out through the mirrored lobby. I checked myself. Each morning, I'd try figuring out if I was plain-looking or plain terrific.

Outside, the morning air felt clear and crisp, tingling deep inside my lungs and awakening a sense of newness. As I turned the corner, a paper plane glided out of the sky with aerodynamic precision. I caught it before a gust of wind took it flying across toward Riverside Park. Words were printed along the crease line: *God cannot be everywhere. That's why He invented mothers.* I smiled up at Mom watching from the third-floor window, then slipped the plane into my jacket pocket and dashed to the Eighty-sixth Street crosstown bus. Twenty minutes to get to the deli before Carolyn had a quadruple chocolate croissant attack.

A single seat near the back of the bus was empty and I grabbed it. In my backpack, somewhere between history notes for my exam this morning and my work planner, was my slim Sony tape recorder. After rewinding the tape, I slipped on the earphones and pushed Play.

The city was waking. People filtered out of their cement cubicles, many on their way to work. Children with schoolbooks hurried along the streets. They were all part of an intricate web into which I was trying to weave my own strand. BRAINS ONLY ON THURSDAY, a sign read from a butcher shop window. I hoped the sign applied only to the lower species in the animal kingdom.

Carolyn's voice on the tape sounded unusually raspy. "I'm going to take chocolate. I'm going to take chocolate," she had threatened after having a fight with her boyfriend, Dillon. He'd called last night after working with his science partner, Lynn Van Der Camp. They were building a model of a single transistor ram cell. He came home filled with ideas about how Carolyn could be more alluring and feminine.

It was almost 7:40. My only hope was that Carolyn hadn't started ravishing a dozen croissants before I got there. She'd lost seven pounds already.

Actually, Carolyn Rolland was my first case ever. Six years ago, we met in Miss Ellen's ballet class for serious study. Our problem was we couldn't be serious and giggled between *grand jetés*. In all the years I've known her, Carolyn's been in constant motion. She's constantly watching her weight, complaining about her hair being too thin, her thighs too fat, always with too many things to do. She's dynamic and unconventional. She's my best friend.

I got off the bus near the deli and went in. Carolyn was on line at the cashier. Her long brown hair cascaded freely over her shoulders and down the back of her blue denim jacket. I could tell by the tightness of her lips that the strain was getting to her. Her eyes looked sad. Inner pain is worse than the other kind because you can't get to it very easily.

I rushed toward her breathlessly, just as she was pulling change from her pocket, paying for the privilege of gaining weight. "No. Put it down!" I screamed. The man at the cash register—he was new—nearly jumped off his stool. Carolyn quickly paid.

"Put it down, you don't need that." I tried to grab the croissant from her hand. She pulled it away.

The cashier at the counter yelled, "Hey, you're getting crumbs all over the floor!" We fought for the croissant until it broke into bits and fell through our fingers. Both of us bent down to pick up the pieces and Carolyn reluctantly threw it into the garbage.

"Don't look so unhappy; that's three hundred calories I saved you. Be glad," I said.

"All this wouldn't have happened if you had gotten here on time," Carolyn whined.

"I'm only five minutes late."

"Well, I've been waiting here twenty minutes."

"Come on."

"Actually," Carolyn confessed, with a slight smile, "I just got here, but what if I *had* been early?"

"Never happened yet," I said. "Let's go."

We headed for school. As we walked, Carolyn pulled out a list of things to do and crossed one off. "What circuitry can he be studying with Van Der Camp?" she asked, disheartened.

"Van Der Camp happens to be his science partner," I tried interjecting some realism. "Why don't you trust him?"

"It would be easier if homework didn't look that attractive," she answered.

"And what are you? Chopped liver? Trust your own electricity!"

"I don't know. He keeps wanting to change me. My hair's not long enough. I talk too fast. My interests change too quickly. And I'm sloppy."

"You're great. And if he doesn't appreciate you, he's crazy!" I said confidently. "You can't keep changing for each boy you go out with. Steve liked a quiet girl. Dillon a chatty one. Soon, a guy wouldn't know who he was taking out. And neither would you. You'd be schizophrenic."

"Oh, Adriana, you make even that sound exciting."

"Just be who you are."

"Absolutely," she said. She turned to me. "Adriana," she asked, in her most vulnerable voice, "who do you think I am?"

We both burst out laughing. Then we stopped. She waited for an answer.

"Well . . . well, you're like no one else on this planet. Unique. One of a kind."

"Keep going," she teased.

"Terrific. Beautiful. Sexy. Warm. Want more?"

"Only if you insist."

We continued walking the last block to school and I thought Carolyn's mind was on the history test that morning. But I was wrong.

"I'm going to do some research in that area," she said decidedly. "In me. It's a little shady right now, but I'm going to sharpen it up. Boy, is it going to knock Dillon's socks off."

"Sounds promising." My eyes lit up. I could see Carolyn was delighted by the possibilities.

"Yep. I think I'm ready to make my statement."

"When? Right now?" I wanted to know.

"Soon. I can feel it."

"Can I help?" I jumped in. "After all, what are friends for?"

Carolyn gazed at me reflectively. "I wish you had someone special, too. Someone to draw you out."

"I have you. And all my cases."

"Oh, I don't mean us." Her lips curved in a smile.

I don't know why, but just then a certain boy flashed across my mind. I'd been seeing him around school lately. I didn't know him, but he was probably the most interesting-looking boy I had seen in a long time. He was handsome, in an unusual sort of way, and intriguing. His face looked vaguely familiar, but we had never spoken a word to each other. I didn't even know his name. I hadn't mentioned him to anyone, not even Carolyn. It was my secret.

The light changed and we crossed the street.

TWO

Jefferson High stood glistening in the early morning sun. The dark red bricks gave the six-story building a sense of substance compared to the grungy tan bricks from the building next door. Although the building was over forty years old and had survived the onslaught of over six hundred high school students each year, it wore its years well.

As we walked inside, the hallway was a bustle of morning activity. A few sofas and chairs were placed around for parents and guests, but we felt this was our lobby, our space. Just then, a strawberry-blond girl in a flowered skirt nearly ran us over.

"Hi, Nellie," I called.

"Nellie?" Carolyn turned to me in surprise. "You mean Nicole."

"No. No, I don't."

"I've known her since third grade. She lives on Seventy-second Street. Her name is Nicole."

"Not anymore," I explained. Carolyn looked confused. "You see, she never was a Nicole really. That was the problem. The name made her feel she had to be sophisticated. Exotic."

"I never thought she was exotic," Carolyn replied.

"Exactly. So last Thursday, when we were sitting around her living room eating pretzel sticks, we changed her name."

"To Nellie?" she asked me.

"Sounds earthy," I insisted. "Nellie!" I called across the

hall. Nellie turned around, jingling some change in her hand.

"Got to call Allen. He's home with the flu. Tell him I'll stop by later with some chicken soup."

I jabbed Carolyn in the elbow. "See? She used to be phony and uptight. See what an Earth Mother she's become? Chicken soup." I stared at Carolyn, making a point.

"Don't look at me. I like my name."

It was now 8:15. More kids were pouring into the lobby. Before class was a good time to touch base.

Abby, who was infatuated with Jonathan, whispered in my ear. "Happiness runs in cycles, and right now I'm on the wash cycle." I couldn't wait for her to move into spin, where she could wring out. She had a habit of acting like she was under water when she was in love.

Jane had a crush on Steve, though her relationships never lasted more than forty-eight hours. And, she always wrote *I.T.A.T.I.* on her book covers. She even had it embroidered on the back of her jacket. "Is That All There Is?"

A typical Monday morning, considering there was a full moon last night. To my left, Miranda was sitting with her saxophone at her side instead of a friend. She didn't seem to mind that. Groups just weren't her thing. I took out my tape recorder and spoke into it quietly. Carolyn was used to it and flipped through her history cards one last time.

Miranda sitting alone. She's separated from the group. That's why she picked the saxophone. Not many girls play it, and she felt it would be all hers. Linda flirting with Tim, but Tim's giving her a hard time. People in love have their share of problems, too. Not having firsthand experience in being in love, it's hard for me to comment personally. Oh. There he is. That boy. God, he's looking this way. He has a camera around his neck. Did something happen to him during the summer? I sort of remember him, but he used to be shorter, plainer. Nondescript. Now he's different. Interesting. More than that. Fantastic. He's looking again. I hope he didn't notice me staring and think I like him. Oh, wait. He was shooting Randy's left foot, which is perpendicular to Trevor Taylor's left foot, so it looks like Randy's got two left feet. When they notice they all laugh. He does seem to have an unusual sense of humor. And an intelligent laugh. Not one of those chuckle kinds or belly laughs. His lips curl up along the ends and his teeth show. A sign he's open. Relaxed. Oh, no. This time he caught me staring. He's coming over. What am I going to do! He stopped a few feet away. With Steve, the editor of the yearbook. Boy, he seems popular. I can see why. Oh, Jane's MUSCLING into the conversation. She's plopped herself down on Trevor's lap. Her last relationship was twelve hours under par.

Jane Mislove, a real live wire. Sweet and all that. Cheerleader. Class representative. Boy collector. But hogs Jefferson's natural resources. I hope she doesn't have an extra foot to offer for Photoplay. *Jane Mislove. Maybe she's missing a little more than love. Ha ha. Names sure are funny. Take Rochelle Firestone. Got two breasts of steel and the heart of a vulture. Not only that, her laugh has a hollow ring to it. The kind one forces for a living. Oops. I think she heard me.*

I slipped the recorder nonchalantly back into my backpack. "Got a problem?" I asked Rochelle. Sometimes people would tell me, but in this case I didn't want to know. Fortunately, she snubbed me and took a walk. The boy with the camera was focusing now on a pair of unassuming topsiders. I looked down at my new white sneakers. If only I wore more expressive shoes. His eyes glanced my way. I looked away again and adjusted my bangs self-consciously. There was something different about him. Not abnormal exactly, but out of the ordinary. Artistic. A touch of the renegade. The way he peered out from the blond hair falling over his eyes. His expression had an aloofness to it, or maybe it was shyness. Sometimes they were too close to call. But his manner was definitely self-contained. Something stirred inside me, making all sense of logic disappear. He continued shooting people's feet! I watched, fascinated.

"Carolyn," I said.

"What?" she asked, still peering down at her history notes.

"See that boy over there? The one with the camera?"

She looked across the room. "Now *that's* a case for you," she said.

"Do you know him?" I asked excitedly.

"Seen him around. With his camera. But show me a person who spends all his time photographing feet and I'll show you a podiatrist in ten years," she said.

"A foot doctor!" I laughed. The thought sounded deliciously absurd. "Well, I think he's cute," I confessed to her for the first time.

"Forget it. Wrong number."

"Why?"

"You're into people and he's into Kodacolor."

"See what you can find out about him." I straightened my shoulders and started to walk away.

"Why are you walking like that?"

"Like what?"

"Like a chair."

"I'm walking straight because it's good for my posture. And I want to make a good impression."

"A piece of lumber doesn't make a good impression unless you happen to be a bench."

"Okay, okay." I relaxed my back. "But see what you can find out."

"Adriana. You're acting weird."

"Nothing serious," I answered, surprised.

In front of us the receptionist posted a notice about an upcoming audition for the junior drama department's production of *Hamlet,* and a photocopy of "Summer in Mount Saint Helens to save the elk." Lauren was reading the audition notice while biting her nails, not that there was much left to bite. I had to find out if she got any sleep last night, so I told Carolyn to go upstairs without me. Then I hurried to catch Lauren. I didn't get two steps before I tripped over my own feet and went flying in the air. A strobe light flashed. I ended up sprawled on the cold speckled tile.

The grinning boy, with his camera, stood over me. "Bumpy ride?" he asked, smiling, snapping away. I lay there speechless, and he began to laugh.

"What's so funny?" I asked, embarrassed, adjusting my green jersey.

"You," he answered.

"Do you always laugh at people who can't walk straight?" I asked, making fun of myself.

"Only if it gets to be a habit." He extended his hand. "Here." He offered to help me up.

But I felt self-conscious. Klutzy. "I can get up myself." With that, I jumped to my feet, but my right ankle buckled under and I tripped again. Even I laughed at the preposterousness. This time I let him grab my hand and pull me up. "Is two times a habit?" I asked, still holding on.

"Who's counting?" he said. "Are you all right?"

I pulled my hand away, then cleared my throat and made cosmetic adjustments. "I've got everything I started with except my pride."

"Oh, that." He smiled at me. "It only gets in the way."

"But I didn't know it affected your balance," I said. Then

I was sorry. What did I say a stupid thing like that for. This was definitely not the way I had imagined meeting him. I'd have looked so much better in my pink sweater, with my hair washed and shiny.

"By the way, my name's Nick," he volunteered.

"Nick," I repeated softly to myself. "It fits." He was the first Nick I had ever met, and his name rolled off my tongue as if I'd said it a hundred times. Then my mind went blank and I didn't know what to say. This was the first time I'd ever been at a loss for words. It scared me. My mind totally shut down.

"Well, gotta be going." I picked up my backpack.

"Do you always rush off like that?" He stopped me.

"Like what?"

"Like that. A whirlwind." His smile was contagious. "I've been watching you."

"You have?" My heart pounded. "But I've got to hand it to you. You're the first person who caught me upside down. In a photo, I mean."

Nick smiled shyly. "Not you. Your feet."

"My feet!"

"I'm always looking for new angles. That was great."

Carolyn did have a knack for astute observations. This guy was weird. "Obviously, then, you missed the best part," I retorted.

"Not to me. Your sneakers say it all."

"They do? What?"

There was a momentary pause. "Your sneakers have *tilt* written all over them."

"Tilt?" I replied, squinting my eyes.

"I'm telling a story without words. Tilt."

"Excuse me, but is this a story about footwear or pinballs?"

He stared into space for a moment. "Call it . . . balance. If your feet feel good, you feel good."

A strange feeling came over me that he was putting me on. I didn't like what I was hearing.

Then he went on. "I think I'm going to program you into my computer. I think you're cute. Keep it going." He focused closer on my feet. "Your feet are so expressive."

"God. Nothing's sacred." I jumped back and forth in constant motion. "Don't you dare!" I screamed.

With that, he lifted his eyes away from the lens long enough to stop snapping. Almost seductively, he spoke, "Can't I even get one of you right side up?"

"No, you may not!" I growled back, then turned to leave.

"Where are you going?" he asked, surprised.

"History test. You make it seem like a treat," I bellowed. "Good-bye."

His golden shock of hair bounced over his forehead. "Wait up. You forgot something." Something made me stop. "You dropped this." He held out my tape recorder. "Never know when you might feel like listening to soft rock."

"Thank you." I grabbed it and walked away. Fortunately, my tape about Miranda and Nick was still locked in place.

"Besides," he called after me, "you forgot to tell me your name."

I paused a moment between the second and third floors. "My friends call me Adriana, but you can call me whatever you want. You obviously will."

"Wait a minute." His voice followed me up the stairs, but I fled to the fifth floor and disappeared through the stairwell door. My knees were shaking. I was out of breath. I ducked into an empty classroom, slipped a fresh cassette into my recorder, and spoke into it.

This person obviously has overwhelming feelings of inferiority, which he thinly disguises behind the lens of a camera, an optic security blanket, or why would he need to see the world through the wrong end of a lens? A jerk. A real jerk. How could I have even thought for a moment that there were possibilities between us? That he was someone I could have liked? Tilt. Really. What an insensitive, pompous bore. Blunt. Too glib for his own good. A twirp of the highest order. It was my mind that was tilted, to think there could have been anything between us. Anything.

I shoved the recorder back into my backpack. One thing I knew for sure: This was not the hour I had wanted to gain when I woke up this morning; rather, I wished it was the hour lost last spring.

THREE

Mr. Wexler sat at his distressed wormwood desk sipping his decaffeinated coffee. He was marking papers at a frantic pace while his eyes darted back and forth across the classroom. He was overseeing the honor system at work.

Carolyn sat diagonally across from me writing her essay at sixty miles an hour. The exam concentrated on couples from the American Revolution: Martha and George, Abigail and her beloved, John Adams. It's true, Mr. Wexler had a fetish with couples through time, charting them from the Cro-Magnon brute to Napoleon and Josephine. If he had been down in the lobby a few minutes earlier, he would have seen prehistoric contact between a certain boy and a girl in a green jersey. I couldn't help but wonder why Mr. Wexler had never gotten married. He was attractive and all that, but maybe he read too much and knew history had a habit of repeating itself. Right at that moment, Mr. Wexler caught me drifting into space, and signaled that I get back to work. "Ten minutes left. You should be on your last question." He tapped his pencil on his mug. I glanced back to my paper, then wondered about that look the foot-snapper had given me. I had a ridiculous desire to see him again. I needed to. I couldn't get his face out of my mind.

After the exam, Lauren squeezed her tall, thin body through rows of desks. "I just became a statistic in the war," she said glumly.

"You probably aced it."

We stepped out through the door. Lauren's voice cracked. "My mother's going to kill me." Her mother did put a lot of pressure on her to succeed. Lauren was visibly upset and pulled me off to the side of the hall. "That horrible thing is happening."

"The move?" I asked sympathetically, my heart dropping.

"After seven moves in eight years, being resilient isn't how well you survive but how fast you can pack." Her eyes teared up. "Dad promised, though, that this would be the last promotion he takes, but he took on an obligation when he signed up as foreign correspondent for the magazine."

I knew how alone she must feel. If I ever had to leave Jefferson High, it would be like dying. But I wanted to be encouraging. "I'll be home at five. Let's talk then," I said, heading off to French class.

As Lauren disappeared through the stairwell door, I took out my tape recorder and began speaking softly into it.

Lauren doesn't know where she'll be next year. Always leaving something behind. Always saying good-bye. I could never do it. Maybe it gets easier each time, but I don't think so. Not from the look on Lauren's face.

A piercing voice interrupted my dictation. "Is the fifty minutes up yet?" The voice was unmistakably Rochelle.

"You should know. You've been eavesdropping." Casually, I slipped the tape recorder out of sight.

"If I really wanted to listen to people's problems, I'd turn on Dr. Ruth." She strutted around me, smirking. Terri and Jerry, nitwits of the highest order, stood closely by her side. "Don't you get tired of taping people's problems?" Rochelle asked. "Don't you have enough of your own?" Jerry and Terri laughed. Rochelle went through friends like Kleenex.

"Don't you get tired of causing them?" I retorted as I grabbed my tape recorder and pushed down to record. *Rochelle's re-duced to invectives. Obviously threatened. Can't wait to find out why. She's exhibiting hostile and aggressive behavior. Makes me wonder why I annoy her so much. Maybe hit a nerve. Explore further.*

With one fast gesture, Rochelle's black ponytail swished around as she returned to her friends. "What a jerk," she remarked. "Tapes got Nixon into a lot of trouble, too."

I talked back into the recorder: *She's big on word salads, too.* With that, Rochelle stormed away, but the scent lingered behind like that of a really cheap perfume.

Next period, I ran down to find Carolyn in the cafeteria. She was munching on a Granny Smith apple and chewing the fat with a few junior girls. Ms. Grover was on lunch duty and set a relaxed, mother-superior tone.

Quickly I ran through the food line and sat down next to Carolyn. "I tell you, 'Rochelle from Hell' is a pipeline. I don't trust her."

"Yeah. She'd turn her mother in for an imported French jacket." Carolyn took another bite, ignoring the kids eating a double portion of ice cream. "Listen. I've found out . . ."

"About Nick?" I cut in.

"You know each other?"

"Past tense. Knew."

"Just thought I'd tell you Dillon is in his English class. Sometimes sees him down in the photo lab. Seems he's a neat guy. Buckley. That's his last name."

"Sssssssh!" I whispered in alarm. "Someone'll hear."

"No one's around." She shrugged her shoulders. Carolyn watched me dig into my beef tacos. "I've been thinking about what you said this morning. About trying too hard to please Dillon. You're absolutely right. I do."

"Ahhah," I wiped some taco sauce off my sleeve.

"Yes. I'm fed up. I'm taking myself off the circuit. Know why?" she asked.

"Why?" I took another bite.

Her eyes widened. "Because it's exhausting, that's why." She leaned over her spartan salad. "And . . . I'm ready to make my statement."

"Really?"

"Yes. I'm going to take a stand. Finally express who I really am." Her attention became diverted. "What's that?" We both listed. "That voice. I know that voice."

We turned to the closed-circuit TV. "Speaking of the devil— look who's there," I squealed. We sat gaping at the monitor— at Rochelle's face.

Courtesy of the video department, the programming brought students up to date on news and happenings around Jefferson. Interesting tidbits. Events. Social comings and goings, like when Mr. Wexler dressed as an aardvark for the Bible as Literature symposium. Things we had to know: "The Political Science Club canceled its meeting this Thursday in order to visit the Manhattan borough president to urge formation of a Youth Advisory Committee. The New York Marathon is taking place the last Sunday of October. Mr. Madden and Ms. Cramie are our joggers-in-residence."

"Seems like she weaseled herself into a new job," I said just as Nick came into the cafeteria and got into the food line. I put down my taco shell. Suddenly, I wasn't hungry anymore.

Carolyn played with a piece of lettuce on her fork, twisting it back and forth into a figure eight. Out of the corner of my eye I could see Nick had gotten a sandwich and milk. He sat on the other side of the room, with a few boys I didn't know.

"You want to make a statement," I said, staring across at Nick. I leaned closer to Carolyn. "Give a circuit-breaker party!"

"A what?" She laughed. "Never been to one."

"Exactly." My eyebrows shifted up and down. My mind began to whirl at the prospect.

"Adriana!" She challenged me. "What are you up to?"

"It's perfect. Break old circuits. Connect new ones."

"You're transmitting. Yes. Yes." She began to cheer.

I was getting excited myself. "Make a statement in a new way. Because you are different, a new person. Everyone will see it. Especially Dillon. Come to a circuit breaker."

"I'm ready. Just plug me in." Carolyn's eyes nearly darted out of her sockets imagining the endless possibilities. "My birthday's next week. Let's break my circuits then."

"We'll do it at lunchtime. Invite all your friends."

"*Only* friends."

"And I'll bring the cake," I happily volunteered.

Rochelle continued broadcasting: "The Oriental Food Sale benefiting Jefferson's costume department for the *Hamlet* production will take place October second, featuring moo shoo pork. Bring lots of yen."

Carolyn and I made faces at each other. "I like her better under glass." Carolyn gave her TV review.

At three o'clock we met outside school to continue planning a party of personal expression. The sun shone brightly. It was one of those rare October days. Unfortunately we couldn't take advantage of it. Carolyn was heading downtown to get her teeth cleaned, which wasn't her idea of fun. But the party was, and we laughed anticipating Dillon's horrified surprise when he realized their circuits were about to be rewired.

Madison Avenue offered its usual share of trendy shops, but this afternoon they held little diversion. My own mind was cutting out. At first, I thought it a mirage on Eighty-first Street. "Look," I screamed.

"Who?" Carolyn squinted her eyes.

"Sssssh. He'll hear you."

"Who?" she boomed out.

"Nick. Over there," I whispered. "In the blue sweater."

Carolyn made a beeline toward him.

"What are you doing? I don't want him to see me."

But Carolyn paid no attention.

"I feel like a spy," I said, catching up. Nick turned into a light tan building, past a sculpture of two robust women. Before I could stop Carolyn, she barreled into the lobby. I wanted to disappear.

"Excuse me," Carolyn asked the doorman. She used her most mature, secure tone—the one she used when we called the 1-800 numbers to see which of us could get a free sample first. Carolyn cleared her throat. "We're delivering a piano and need to check the floor. Buckley. 6B?"

"You mean 18D," he let slip out. "But if it's a baby grand, you're in trouble. The last baby grand didn't fit in the elevator."

"Upright," Carolyn managed before running out of the lobby in hysterical laughter.

Not until we crossed the street did I realize where she was dragging me—into a flower shop.

"Oooh, no," I shrieked.

"Why not?"

"Boys never get flowers."

"Where have you been!"

"I don't even like him."

"Yes you do," she said. "Go ahead. Admit it." She egged me on.

I didn't answer.

She reached into her pocket and counted her money. "I can spare two dollars toward this relationship. Not a penny more. What about you?"

I pulled out a dollar and some change.

"That's all it's worth?"

"That's all I've got!"

The flower shop smelled like August in Martha's Vineyard. We poked around.

"What's that one called?" I asked the salesperson, pointing to a long-stemmed orange flower that seemed slightly askew.

"Bird of paradise." He admired it. "Lives a long time."

"How much is it?" I asked.

"Who cares?" Carolyn blurted out. "Live dangerously. We'll take two."

"One," I corrected her.

He began wrapping the strangely configured flower. "That'll be four dollars."

"Oh," I said, disappointed. We counted our change. We were twenty cents short.

He smiled. "That fine, miss."

Carolyn handed me a card. "Write something."

I began to think. "No. I'll let the flower speak for itself," I said, admiring the exotic burst and whimsical shape. The salesman had now wrapped the improbable messenger in clear plastic and held it out.

"Do you deliver?" I asked.

"One flower?" He cringed from shock, then shook his head.

"One flower's worth a thousand words," Carolyn read from a poster on flowergrams pasted on the wall.

"Just across the street?" I begged.

He peered out his glass storefront.

"There." I pointed to Nick's building.

He thought a moment. "All right," he agreed reluctantly with a slight smile. He seemed to enjoy playing Cupid.

"What'd I just do?" I hit myself on the head as he closed the door behind us.

"You made an opening bid. It's daring. It's bold. It's you," she said, putting her hand on my shoulder.

I had to smile. "Yes. Maybe it is."

"See how you always make me late? The dentist is going to yell, and I'll have to tell him it's your fault."

"Blame it all on me. I don't care," I said throwing my hands up in the air, feeling gloriously happy.

"Well, you don't want plaque to stand in the way of my finding out who I am, do you?" she said, adjusting her coat collar.

"Absolutely not," I replied. "Say, Carolyn, do you believe in hate at first sight?"

FOUR

"Adriana." I heard my brother calling from the next room. "The phone's for you." Then he returned to his TV program.

Miranda had barely said hello when she was interrupted by a pizza delivery. While waiting for her to pay the delivery boy, I stood there watching Richard absorbed in a Giants' football game. The house seemed empty. Mom and Dad were at a Jasper Johns exhibition at the Museum of Modern Art, but my father would have been happier sitting with Richard watching the game. Not that Dad cared that much about football, but he loved being with Richard, especially now that Richard was away at college. He came home from Brown on sporadic weekends and holidays. Actually, I think Richard was a little homesick, the way he'd walk around the living room like he was discovering parts of the house for the first time. Meta-perspective. I read about that in a book. That's when you think about what someone else is thinking about. And right now I'm thinking about Richard and how we used to vie for our parents' attention. But now Richard had to go away to school and I got both our shares. It's like my parents were doing double time on me just when they should have been letting up.

Miranda returned to the phone breathlessly. "Got to make it fast. The pizza'll get cold."

"Listen, Miranda, Carolyn's thowing a circuit-breaker party next Thursday. In the cafeteria.

"What's that?"

"She's getting ready to really express herself. Can you help?"

"Sure. But how?"

"Play something on your saxophone. Set the right mood."

She giggled. "If you can take it, so can I. What?" she asked modestly.

"How about 'When the Saints Go Marching In'?"

"Doesn't sound good as a solo. Needs percussion."

"Ask someone."

"Well, there's Alex," she said in a sweet voice. "But he talks mostly to the string section."

"See if he's interested in a duet."

"I can't do that."

"Why not?"

"Because we don't talk to each other."

"You can fix that easy. Music is the language of love. Just ask him."

"I don't know. He warms up with some other kids."

"Miranda, you have your own way of warming up."

"A nice way of saying I don't fit in."

"You're just different. Nice different," I said supportively. "There are kids who don't understand a person like you. Kind. Sensitive. Gentle."

"You mean out of it," Miranda moaned.

"Look, next time you have band practice, say hello, and play the hell out of your saxophone. Make the kettledrum stand up and take notice."

"All right. I'll try. Gotta get back to my pizza now—and my book. Agatha Christie. Bought it on the remainder shelf for a dollar. I'll give it to you when I'm finished."

"Great. But don't tell me the ending."

"That was your fifth call in an hour," Richard advised me as he reached for another handful of nacho chips.

"Some people have their saxophone. Others, their telephone."

He shook his head like an older brother.

"Well, what are friends for?" I asked him rhetorically, munching on a chip. "And by the way, Carolyn's calling me back after her bath."

Carolyn did call back briefly to go over the invitation list, and we decided to order a cake shaped like a free spirit. Carolyn was working on the design. The bakery said she had till Tuesday morning to bring in the sketch. We agreed on vanilla sponge inside with as much butter cream frosting as was humanly possible.

"Are you going to ask Nick?" she asked.

"Of course not."

Jane Mislove called in. She had a date with a new boy whom she had met at the copy shop that morning when she was duplicating a paper on the importance of the mayfly in our society, which she subtitled "Lasts for One Brief Moment, Then Kaput." Tim called in quickly, wondering what I thought of his taking Sara to the laser show at the planetarium. I told him that it sounded great.

Later that night there was a knock on my door. Richard poked his head in. "Hey, Adriana, got a minute?"

"Sure, if you don't mind sleep-talking," I said, sitting up in bed. I stared at him. "Is something wrong?"

"No," he said, backing off, changing his mind. "You were sleeping?"

"Listen, if I were sleeping, I wouldn't be talking." But he stood there silently, very still. My curiosity was piqued and I begged him, "Now I'll really never be able to sleep unless you tell me what it is."

The red swivel chair seemed too small for his five-foot-ten frame, but he didn't seem to mind.

"I was just thinking about you."

"About me?" I answered, surprised. "Why?"

"I was just wondering where you were in all of this," he said, turning to me.

"In all of what?" I asked, taken aback by his question.

"Well . . . I just worry about you sometimes." He spoke gently, like he really meant it.

"Richard." I beamed, touched by his concern.

He sat there balancing on two wheels of the chair. After an interminable pause, I couldn't take it anymore. "Are you a man or a mouse? Squeak up!" I said.

"It all doesn't sit right," he said.

"What?"

"You know what I'm talking about."

"No, I don't."

"When are you going to stop living everyone else's life?" he blurted out.

I didn't say anything, just smoothed the comforter down around me tightly and puffed up the pillows under my head. "Listen, I'm falling asleep. It's getting late."

"Sure," he said, rising to his feet. "But I hope you wake up soon, little sister." He called good-night before closing the door behind him.

Alone in the darkness, I grabbed my pillow. Tears began to roll down my face. With all my friends, all the people I knew, why did I feel so very much alone?

FIVE

José Ramirez, the sanitation engineer for the school building, pointed me in the direction of the photo lab, a turquoise door at the end of the corridor.

The room was still. Plastic bottles, negative strips, and prints were stacked along the sides on shelves. On the bulletin board a note was pinned up: *Jim, call Lou about tickets to the Guggenheim.* Student schedules were underneath, and below these was a sign written in a bold black marker: DO NOT DISTURB THE DUST. That made me feel right at home. Too much cleanliness was bad for the nervous system.

Then Nick's voice came out from the dark. "Be out in a jiffy." I froze. Old rules flew out the window—be calm, analytic, collected. Instead, I panicked. Nick appeared from behind the curtain and, without looking up, began to speak. "Mr. Saultern. It's a little underexposed." He held the negative up to the light like flypaper.

"Hello," I said, cutting in. "No one is here but me."

He appeared surprised. "Adriana!"

"I ummm . . . ummm . . . Dillon Porter mentioned he might be down here. Do you know him? I lied.

"Yes, but he's not here till fifth period."

I smiled self-consciously. "Actually, it was you I was really looking for," I admitted.

"Really?"

"Yes . . . I . . ."

Right then a buzzer went off, and he returned to the dark-room. "You can come," he said and invited me along.

As I bumped into a washbasin, I thought, How can I be such a klutz, especially around him?

"You'll get used to it," he said gently. We were in total darkness except for an amber light.

"Safelight," he explained. "Just enough light to see what you're doing without knocking the development out of kilter."

I stood there waiting for my eyes to catch up with his. He started banging a metal tray.

"Making nouvelle cuisine?" I asked, watching him move around like a chef.

"Air bubbles ruin the soufflé." And he gave the tray another bang. "Just adding a little agitation to this concoction." Then he handed me a metal lid. "Hold this a minute."

"Too many cooks . . ."

But he interrupted. "Two is never too many down here."

I wondered if he could like me, too. "Nick . . . ," I began, finding enough courage, "Carolyn's birthday is next Thursday. I don't think you know her, but she's my best friend. Long brown hair. Very pretty." Just then my nose twitched. "Ammonia?" I asked, trying to decipher the scent.

"Phenidone." He pulled out a reel of film. "I love the smell."

"You must be chemically gifted," I said, watching him immerse the dripping film into yet another tray. " . . . And we're having a party for her in the cafeteria . . . ," I continued. "Will you . . ."

"Yes," he interrupted me before finishing.

"You will?"

"Why not?" He smiled at me.

"Then you'll take the pictures?"

"Oh." He seemed disappointed.

"It's not that. I want you to come, too. But we wanted the party documented. His eyes crinkled up at the ends as he smiled faintly, then dropped the film into a third pan.

"A bath," he explained. "You can help me count. One chimpanzee. Two chimpanzee."

"How may chimps do we need?"

"Sixty would fix the image just fine."

My attraction to him increased as the numbers went up. I felt this unexplainable pull and a shortness of breath that wasn't from chemicals, at least not the kind in bottles. And we had counted only to twenty-three. This chemical reaction caught me off guard. I wondered if he felt the same. The air hung differently between us now, and the counting got slower and slower. By the time we reached thirty chimpanzees, I realized that Nick wasn't half bad. And I was beginning to half like him. "So quiet down here," I whispered.

We stared at each other in silence, then laughed at our awkwardness. "My photography instructor, Mr. Saultern, says silence can be the best form of conversation." He moved closer.

"I see what he means," I replied, moving closer, too. I watched as he stuck a finger into the rapidly running water as if taking its temperature. Then he placed a clothespin over the top of the negative strip and hung it up to dry before tiptoeing out. I followed. "Dust," he explained. My eyes adjusted to the change of light in the outer room.

"What kind of pictures did you want?" he asked.

"It's Carolyn's circuit-breaker party."

He laughed, amused. "What circuit is she breaking."

"You'll have to come and photograph it to find out."

"Sounds intriguing." He set the timer in the outer room for twenty minutes. "Here. Let me show you what I do." He lifted a stack of eighty-by-ten-inch photos from the metal desk.

I flipped through the photos. "They're all feet!" I exclaimed.

"Yes," he said proudly. "That's my thing."

"Don't you do head shots?" I asked, more for Carolyn's sake than mine. "Candids?" He didn't answer my question. "Mr. Saultern's submitting me for this contest where they pick ten kids in the whole country for a photographic safari in Africa. It's led by a former student of Edward Steichen's. He was a famous photographer. He's dead now." He watched me flip through the pile on my lap. "I'm calling it 'Portrait of an American Sole.' Like it?"

"Oh, yes, very catchy," I said enthusiastically, flipping through the rest. I almost felt his shoulder touching mine.

"I like walking in their shoes," he explained. "See what it's like." Then he pointed out his favorites. "A penny loafer with a buffalo-head nickel—1937 D. Three-legged. I call it 'Made in America. Save in America.' Actually, the nickel's worth more than the shoe," he added. "Wedgies. Oxfords. See these sandals? I call it 'Airing out your toes on a sunny evening.' Cowboy boots. Ski boots. Sneakers of every variety." One even had no shoes at all. "That foot's got every curve in the human body," he said playfully, running his finger along the outline. "That's why it's titled 'The Naked and the Flesh.' "

I shook my head, slightly embarrassed. No foot had gone unnoticed. I smiled into his blue eyes.

"Even calluses can be expressive. Heel spurs. Hammer-toes."

"You're really into feet, aren't you?"

"Oh, I've done candids, too. There was a time if you had a face, I'd shoot it. But now I want to create a new relationship with a part of the body that has gone hidden for years."

The more he spoke, the more intriguing he became.

"Look at that," he continued as he singled out a girl wearing high-heeled shoes on what seemed to be a country road. " 'If the shoe fits, don't wear it.' "

"I'd say she wasn't interested in the walking part." I studied the picture. "Who'd wear high-heeled patent leather shoes to go fishing?"

"Exactly. Shoes say a lot about a person's intentions. Do you like fishing?" he asked me.

"Bass and trout. I wear sneakers, of course." My hand flipped to the best photo—a symmetrical pair of dotted sneakers, perfectly laced and pristine clean.

"Those're Rochelle Firestone's feet. Do you know her?" he asked me.

"Let's say I know a neurotic sneaker when I see one," I replied.

"Sounds like you don't like her."

"Do you?" I asked.

He didn't answer. The buzzer went off, and Nick dashed into the other room. I trailed behind, watching him place a negative under the enlarger. After turning a few knobs and focusing, he called out, "There it is!" We watched an image forming on a piece of shiny blank white paper.

"Oh, let me see," I begged, trying to peer over his shoulder.

"No, no." He pushed me away. "Developing takes time. It can't be rushed." Slowly, very slowly, the picture appeared before us. "Why, it's a shoe!" I exclaimed.

"Of course." He took the paper out. "What would you call this?" he asked, interested in my response.

"Oh," I quipped happily, "an off-beat projective technique." I smiled, then studied the photo more closely. I wanted to put my best psychological foot forward. "Shadows. More dark than light," I began slowly.

"And . . ." he offered encouragingly.

"Laces mixed up. Person on the sloppy side. Yes, definitely. A little pigeon-toed, too." I tried being serious but instead burst into hysterics. It all seemed so silly, but I was having fun. "Look at those toes. Curling up at the edges. God," I said, looking up at him, "this shoe's a real mess. I'd call it 'A Pure and Simple Misfit.' "

He shook his head, listening. "It doesn't have a mate—did you notice that?" he asked.

"Oh, yes. True. True." I had to agree. "Wait a minute!" I began getting into it. "No vivid colors. Bland."

"That's because the picture's black and white."

"What are you doing, playing the sneaker's advocate?" I said accusingly.

"Needs a little lightening up. Takes things so seriously. Don't you think?" Nick said.

"Absolutely. You know, I feel sorry for that shoe." I shrieked at the preposterousness of it all, nearly falling over. "I'm changing it to 'Help Needed: Inquire Within.' "

By now we were both holding our sides, almost rolling off our chairs. "The shoe needs surgery!" I declared.

He continued laughing. "That's your foot you're sending into surgery."

"I'd know my own foot," I said between gasps. "We've been connected for years."

"Oh?"

Just the way he said that, his expression, made me take another look. Suddenly, I wasn't laughing anymore.

He was right. It *was* my foot. I looked up at him, hurt. "So is that what you think of me? A heavy, serious mess? That requires surgery?"

"You said that. Not me."

"You were making fun of me, weren't you?"

"Come on, Adriana. Lighten up. We were just having a few laughs."

"It's a cheap shot!"

"The camera doesn't lie. Besides, we were just having fun."

"At my expense." I turned away.

"Adriana," he tried apologizing, "it's just my way. Can't I express myself through a portrayal?"

"Betrayal is more like it." I turned back, tossing the newly developed photo into the trash. "You and your camera. Both work on automatic," I lashed out before storming toward the door.

He tried stopping me. "Is that something you picked up off the shelves at Barnes and Noble?" He put his hands on the door.

My face turned red. "Yes, it is. It's called 'Photo Analysis for the Lunatic.' Have you read it?"

He moved closer. "Why do you think I want to photograph your feet?"

"Because you have a foot fetish. How should I know why?"

"Because it's the only way to make you stand still."

A long row of negatives hung along the wall drying. I tried not to brush against them, but who cared about negatives or upsetting the dust. "In case you haven't noticed," my voice quivered, "it isn't just those prints that are underdeveloped!" Then I ran out the door, nearly knocking over Rochelle. She was standing there, perfect to the last mohair.

"Going somewhere?" she asked.

"None of your business."

"Well, there's one person in there who isn't interested in your services, Miss Shrinko."

"Has anyone ever told you that your feet are unphotogenic?" I blurted out. And with that, I ran up three flights of stairs to my locker. Math was next period, and I needed my binder for class. While I ran, I kept scolding myself for going to that photo lab in the first place. Someone else could have taken the pictures. Miranda has a Minolta, or I could have used my old reliable Kodak Disc. It had been a mistake going down there. But as Freud says, there are no accidents.

SIX

The party was gaining momentum during fourth period. Carolyn was determined to make this a party to end all parties, and I was determined to help. There was no limit to Carolyn's imagination. The centerpieces, made of futuristic tomato plants, fascinated even Lynn Van Der Camp, the botany specialist. She took her tray and sat across the room eyeing them. Needless to say, she hadn't been invited. Oblong tables defined our space, and Lynn was definitely on the other side. So was Rochelle.

Carolyn shone radiantly in a lovely dress we had found last Saturday at the Amsterdam Attic thrift shop. It was fuchsia, with wide, expressive sleeves. And the pink orchid I had given her was pinned in her hair as if she were a girl from Bora Bora.

Closer to the food, Miranda played the saxophone, mostly jazz pieces but mixed with some oldies but goodies. The whole atmosphere had a slight touch of the bizarre. Linda and Sara had borrowed lobster outfits from the costume department, and Steve Foster had gotten hold of some stilts. It was captivating. If Carolyn didn't get a job as a weatherperson, as she wanted to, she could always find work as a party planner.

I kept glancing at the door, hoping Nick would walk in—even though I couldn't stand him. Dillon watched the antics while he nibbled on sour-cream dip and taco chips. His black hair seemed to float around his face like a wild chocolate soufflé. I sensed a slight tension. So far, Dillon hadn't a clue to what the theme of the party was, only that Carolyn was in a wildly devilish mood, and his antennas were up, alert.

"Doesn't she look beautiful?" I asked, watching him watch her across the tables.

"Mmmm," he murmured. "Did she cook all this food herself?"

I nodded proudly.

The teacher on lunch duty, Mrs. Moskowitz, sat mesmerized at the other end of the room, observing with an incredulous expression. Thank goodness we had gotten approval from the dean of students. Everyone we had invited was here, except Nick. But who cared? After all, no one missed him. I walked over to Lauren, who looked like she needed to talk. She had been in deep conversation moments before with a group of girls. "Should I take the part of Ophelia or not?" she asked.

"Lauren. To play the part of someone going mad? Are you kidding? I'd jump at the chance."

"But she goes mad from love. Because Hamlet doesn't want her anymore. He's got his own problems. And what happens if my father has to move in the middle?"

"Listen, Lauren, you can't put your life on hold."

"Maybe we *will* still be here by June."

Just then I noticed a boy grab a frying pan from the kitchen and join Miranda in the next set. Miranda smiled shyly through her dark bangs, and I knew immediately it had to be Alex, the kettledrum boy. I began tapping to the beat of the now two-piece jazz ensemble when a strobe light nearly blinded me.

"Nick!" I gulped.

"That was a good shot." He advanced the film, pleased.

"You decided to come!"

"You invited me, didn't you?"

"Well . . . yes . . . but . . ."

He grinned. "I just brought a few rolls of high-speed film, that's all. Just in case you go into fast forward again."

I smiled back. "I hope you won't have to use them."

"I like to be prepared for anything."

"I'm sorry for what I said the other day. I didn't mean most of it."

"Me, too."

With Carolyn's jubilant mood, Dillon's wary look, and Nick at my side, electricity was in the air. We wandered around the room while Nick shot away. Then I dragged him over to the birthday cake in the center of the room. I could tell he was amazed by the piano keys along the crescent edge of the cake and the pink butter-cream girl swirling up from middle C. Just then Lauren whizzed by. "Thanks for that advice," she called to me. "I'm really leaning in that direction." Then she continued on.

Nick turned to me. "What's all that about?"

"A case."

"A case of what?"

I took his black film canister and shook it up and down. "We all have our cases, don't we?"

He smiled and grabbed the case back. "Do we?" We stared into each other's eyes, unaware that a crowd had gathered around Carolyn, who was standing on top of a Formica table, her arms extended. Slowly and deliberately, she began to sing.

> *I'm better than ever.*
> *Better than ever.*
> *I need you so much*
> *I have found*
> *myself.*

The kids began crowding around the table. Carolyn was pouring her whole self into this song.

As much as I loved Carolyn, her voice was not one of her strongest features. I mean, she really liked singing and all that. However, she was slightly off key and a little flat. But singing made her happy, and she seemed very happy right then and didn't much care how she sounded. After all, this was her party. But it was driving Dillon crazy.

"Sssssh!" he indicated to her with his finger, trying to shut her up. But she wasn't getting his signals. If anything, it only made her sing louder. "Has she lost her marbles?" he asked me. "God, does she stink," he said, holding his ears, but I think he was more upset that he couldn't control her. He covered his eyes from embarrassment. But no one else felt embarrassed for her. They were enjoying it.

Only Rochelle seemed to be making faces. When she got up with Louis the Ape, I thought they were leaving. They brought their trays to the garbage. Next thing I knew, Rochelle was heading in our direction with a bowl of warm spaghetti. Before I could stop her, Rochelle dumped the bowl of spaghetti right over Carolyn's head.

The music came to a crashing halt. Kids stood speechless. Carolyn was stunned. She just stood there on top of the Formica table, spaghetti slowly dripping through the pink orchid in her hair, curling down her fuchsia dress. Without another thought, I grabbed what was left of the spaghetti in the bowl. "You didn't finish your lunch," I said, hurling it right at Rochelle. "Enjoy!" I added.

"Food fight!" yelled Dillon and doused Louis the Ape with mustard. Jane added some tuna salad, so he looked like an open-face sandwich.

It was a real free-for-all. Nick snapped away, stopping only to wipe yogurt from his lens.

Bells started ringing, and Mrs. Moskowitz stormed in, this time with Ms. Grover and a few other faculty members. Whistles blew as they rounded us up. But as they did, I could hear Carolyn's voice through the crowd.

Better than ever.
I'm better than ever.

SEVEN

Nick was sitting right next to me in detention hall. We all felt sticky and smelled like a refrigerator that had been turned off for days. String beans, spaghetti, yogurt, and baked ziti clung to our hair and clothes. I tried pulling some beef and barley off my shirt. Carolyn was a wreck. Yet, from her expression, she seemed perfectly content. Dillon had to have gotten the message.

We were being called in to see Mrs. Crumper one at a time. Nellie. Rochelle. Louis the Ape. Even the Lobster Twins. Lauren was biting her nails.

Nick came out smiling. "I enjoyed it," he told me reassuringly. "I told her people want me to photograph them for the same reason they go to a shrink or a gypsy. Find out who they really are."

"She must have thought you were crazy." I laughed.

"Who cares," he said matter-of-factly, and headed back to class.

Then Carolyn marched in, and when she walked out of Crumper's office, her head was held high and proud. "At least I am who I am," she said defiantly. "Don't worry, I told Crumper that even though you helped me plan the entire party, it was all my idea. So I got you off the hook."

"Carolyn. Don't try and take this rap yourself."

My turn was next. As I walked slowly toward her office, I

heard Crumper repeating over and over, "They're adolescing again! They're adolescing again!"

Mrs. Crumper was hovering over a ten-gallon aquarium, dangling wilted lettuce in front of a snail. "Come in." Her tone contradicted her words.

"Take a nap," she ordered the snail as if the snail was planning to whoop it up. School reports and college applications were strewn across her desk. So was my manila folder. How could my whole life squeeze into a legal-size manila folder when I had a hard time fitting all I could into each day?

"Sit down. It won't stunt your growth," she directed. She wanted to take a load off her feet, too. Her brown hair was pulled back tightly in a knot and it accentuated her heavy jowls.

"What are you doing now?" she said accusingly.

"Nothing," I said innocently.

"Nothing doesn't cause a near-riot." She used her quiet, threatening voice. "See that sign over there?" She pointed to an official document in a thin black frame.

"Yes," I replied, staring at it.

"Do you know what that is?"

"A license?" I replied.

"It took me years of night school." She winced, probably reliving the entire experience.

"Nice," I replied.

Then she leaned over, resting on her elbows. "You're not supposed to practice without a license. It's a state law. And I'm the one who's certified here!" Crumper explained.

"I know that. But maybe some kids feel more comfortable coming to me." She didn't like that remark.

Crumper swiveled around in her chair. "Let's cut the garbage and get to the bottom line." I looked at her innocently.

"Come on. I know all about it," she said. "Rochelle was in here. Telling me what happened. That you were behind this circuit-breaker fiasco!"

"What fiasco?" I asked.

"Do I speak a foreign language?"

"But Carolyn had a statement to make."

"Then let *her* make it! You know, you're driving me crazy," she said.

"Carolyn needed to express herself. It was good for her. And I don't regret helping. Unfortunately, Rochelle has absolutely no ear for music."

"I don't care if Carolyn was discovered by Hollywood talent scouts. And while we're on it, you've got Lauren confused. She doesn't know if she's coming or going. And Miranda's mother called and told me you told Miranda to go out to a rock concert, and she was in such a daze from the crowd she called her mother in a panic."

"The music was probably too loud for her. Besides, Miranda never goes out at night. It seemed like a good idea."

"Would you tell her to jump off a bridge to overcome her fear of heights?"

"Of course not. What do you think?"

"Don't ask. Listen. I'll make a deal. You handle the big stuff like who runs for president. Politics in the Middle East." She swiveled toward me. "Let me handle the small stuff, like Tim cutting school for a week to gamble in Atlantic City. Or Alison Warner's burnout. Small things." She took out a peppermint from her desk and offered me one. I politely refused. The thought crossed my mind that the candy was laced with sodium pentothal.

"Carolyn's problems are my problems. Big or small."

"Listen, you. Do you know how much current your brain

can lose sitting out your junior year? I know this statement stuff was your idea," she said accusingly, as her voice rose, "and I don't like it. And that boy. Nick. The one with the aggressive camera technique."

"I think he's really sensitive."

"There you go again. No one asked for your unprofessional opinion."

"And Lauren feels dislocated and Miranda's shy."

"Send them to me."

"They can't talk to you. That's why there are oranges and apples."

"Fine. You become an apple and get your degree."

"See. You speak in metaphors. That's why some kids can't talk to you."

"Enough!" she hissed.

"You're getting upset."

"Damn right, I am. You exasperate me."

"Calm down. It's not good for your blood pressure."

"I'm the counselor here. I'll calm down when I want to calm down. What am I going to do with you?"

Just then, the phone rang. A concerned father called about the pros and cons of Boston Unviersity. Unfortunately, from my point of view she sounded well informed. She hung up and turned to me. "I might just have to call your parents in before report day," she warned sternly. "Sources tell me you were writing a term paper for Linda Lerner. In the cafeteria," she said.

"I wasn't writing it for her. I was merely jotting down her thoughts. She thinks best when she's in a dreamlike state. Eyes closed. Sees things in images, she's so brilliant."

"I see. And you're simply translating it into English."

"That's all."

"You know, you could do real damage." She glared at me. "You've got precious little in the upper story when it comes to technique. A trained person knows you can't tear away a person's foundation until they have something pretty solid to replace it with."

She didn't stop. "My job is to get you kids through four years of Jefferson and into college. And unfortunately, that includes you."

"I know I don't know all the answers. Or maybe even half. But I can be there if someone needs me."

She started twisting back and forth in her chair. "Look, one thing is certain, a sixteen-year-old girl should be most concerned with getting out of her teens with the least amount of pain." She yanked out a book and began to read. " 'Adolescence—coming in like a child, going out like an adult.' " She looked at me. "I guess coming in like a child is universal. But going out like an adult can't be guaranteed."

I was beginning to get angry. "I stick by my friends and nothing can change that."

She walked to the window, then turned toward me. "Look, I want it to stop. Now! No more taping cases. Do you get it, Greenhorn?"

I nodded, agreeing just to get her off my back.

"And if I can give you some free advice." She spoke in a slow, deliberate voice. "Therapy begins at home."

"Yes, Mrs. Crumper."

"I've got another meeting now. But consider this a warning. I won't put it on your record. Not this time. But one more breakout . . . Send the nuts and free spirits to me and get on with your *own* life," she said as she closed the door.

Once out of the room, I sighed with relief.

"Adriana," I heard a voice call.

"Nick! I thought you went to class."

"I came back to see how you fared in the torture chamber."

I didn't reply, simply made a face.

"Hey." He tried cheering me up. "Don't let her get you down. You've got spunk, kid."

"That might be all I have when she finishes with me."

"I doubt that." His conviction was reassuring. Then his eyes drifted. "What's that!" He startled me.

"What?" I jumped.

"On your shoulder strap!" He pointed.

Carefully, I slipped the backpack off. Peeking back at me was Mrs. Crumper's snail friend, crawling along the black shoulder strap. "He's running away from home," I said and laughed, cupping him in my hand. "He doesn't need a guidance counselor either."

"Can I?" Nick extended the palm of his hand and I placed the snail in it. Nick tapped the spiral shell. The snail slowly poked its head out and he stroked it. I watched his gentleness.

"Want to go to the park this afternoon? Give him his freedom?" I asked bravely.

"Why not?" He smiled as he let the snail explore the inner part of his lower arm.

Each of the other times we had met had started pleasantly, too. But were we like the mayfly or the coho salmon, I wondered, which get along for one brief moment and then flicker out? Over? A part of me was frightened, almost terrified, to find out, and yet I decided he was worth the risk. "Meet me in the lobby at three," I said, taking a deep breath.

EIGHT

Before school let out, I met Carolyn in the girls' room. She was rubbing a few spots on her fuchsia dress while I peeled a few tomato seeds from my shirt. We officially declared the party a triumph, and then I told her about Nick. "Carolyn, I think I really like him." She continued fanning away but I knew she had heard.

At the sound of the three-o'clock bell, I ran down to the lobby and checked myself again in the lobby's art display case. No use. Dark strands of hair were greasy with pasta sauce and congealing in clumps.

The usual din in the lobby at three o'clock was just a murmur. All I could hear was my heart racing out of control. I tried deep breathing for increased relaxation, but while I was exhaling Nick came up from behind.

"Getting in touch with the muse?" he asked wryly.

I forgot about breathing altogether as we turned and headed toward Madison Avenue.

A slight breeze ruffled our hair as we talked and laughed, and before we knew it, we were in Central Park. He looked even more attractive in natural light, the way it highlighted his blue eyes and accented the golden tones of his skin. It was the first time I had seen him up close out-of-doors.

We stood watching a few wiry squirrels jumping from one precarious limb to another playing a game of tag, teasing each other with a nutty morsel. How nice it was to be with Nick;

it was just the kind of day on which you could really enjoy being with the right person. I watched his almond-shaped eyes crinkle when he smiled, as if delicious thoughts danced inside. I wanted him to share them with me, especially his private thoughts. It was like watching a foreign movie with subtitles. And, although he hadn't taken one shot since we left school, I might just as well have been walking with a moving camera. He began humming a tune as we walked. "I'm better than ever. Better than ever." And we both broke out laughing. A honey-colored Airedale came around and sniffed. Nick bent over, petted him. "Do you have a dog?" he asked.

"No. Do you?"

"No. But I have twenty animal cages in my bathroom. Boa constrictor. Gecko, iguana, chameleons. A few crickets."

"All in your bathroom?" I asked incredulously.

"And a crawfish missing a claw. It's regenerating a new one."

"A boa?" I asked.

"Well, actually, I did until two years ago when my mother ran into the boa in the shower. He used to like wrapping himself around the shower rod. You should have heard her scream 'One of us has to go!' Unfortunately, I had to get rid of the wrong one."

He made me laugh. "Miranda loves reptiles, too. She wants to be a veterinarian."

"Who's Miranda?"

"A case of mine. She played the saxophone at the party."

"You and your cases." He grabbed his camera and began photographing the dog playing with a 7-Up can. "I like his feet. All four of them." He rewound the finished roll and quickly loaded a new roll. During that time, I reached into my pocket and made sure the snail was still there.

The lake opened up in front of us. There were a few rowers enjoying the last warm days of fall.

"Perfect!" Nick exclaimed, quickening his pace.

"Think he'll be happy there?"

"Adriana, he's only a snail."

"But he's got feelings, too."

The snail poked his head out from his shell as if to confirm it. Two tiny antennae vibrated upward.

"The nervous system of a snail is very underdeveloped," Nick offered knowingly.

Side by side, we walked past the boat house and onto a small peninsula. It felt strange with Nick by my side, but strangely nice. This time, I caught Nick staring at me. Maybe Freud was right. Love and hate are close friends. A thin line, a simple conversation, perhaps even a snail can change a person's life forever.

Crimson red and yellow leaves twirled lazily down from a sturdy oak and caught themselves on Nick's jacket.

"Here," I said, removing a leaf from his shoulder. I twisted it by its stem so the colors blended together like a top. My mind was whirling, too.

"Did you live in the city all your life?" I asked.

He shook his head. "My first few years we lived in Brazil."

"Your first words were in Portuguese!"

"That is, until I was four and we moved to Kenya. *Arros con pollo* became *kuky na nazi*. That's chicken and rice.

"Kenya, like in Africa?"

"Near Amboseli Game Reserve. My father was an environmentalist," he explained. "Mostly animal migration."

"Imagine growing up in the wild."

"This city's pretty wild, too." He laughed at the thought. "But not as wild as the frenzied bongos in mating season."

My interest was aroused. "And what season is that?"

"Any season before noon." We both laughed.

"The farthest I've ever gotten is Sanibel Island. That's off the coast of Florida."

"Oh. A shell safari?" He smiled.

"Yes. Scallops mostly. A few starfish." Then I turned toward him. "Someday, though, I'm going to travel all over the world. I want to see everything. Everything. That's a promise I've made to myself."

"My father was a traveler."

"Was?" I asked, surprised. "You mean he doesn't travel anymore?"

He spun around in his tracks. "What's this? Twenty questions?" he asked defensively. "I thought you were off duty."

I was hitting a raw nerve. "Sorry," I apologized.

We walked for a minute or two in silence. Nick kicked a small gray rock a few yards ahead. "I said 'was' 'cause he's not my father anymore." His voice became quiet, almost inaudible, and surprisingly devoid of feeling. It gave me goose bumps.

"Not your father anymore?"

The next kick sent the rambling pebble disappearing behind a thorny bush. "He left us," he said. "That's when we came back to New York, Mom and I." A few small veins in his temple seemed protruded, pulsating. I could almost see the blood pumping through his body. We just kept walking through the bushes until I could be silent no longer.

"But a boy needs a father," I said sympathetically.

His focus seemed far away. Almost out of reach. "The water is that way." He directed us through a side path.

"Do you ever see your father?" I continued. All I heard was our own footsteps over crunching leaves.

"I can see how your friends get sucked into this. All these questions."

I didn't respond.

"How many cases do you have? Two? Three?" He wanted to know.

"Nine. Active ones. Others, too."

"Just keep your mitts off me."

"Nick. I know how to separate business from pleasure."

"Good. Because I don't want to go out with a case worker."

"Don't worry. You're safe."

"Now, let's talk about you."

"Me?" I said. "Oh, nothing very interesting. Grew up on Long Island. Moved into Manhattan for Dad's work. He's a criminal lawyer. Lots of lawsuits. Married Mom while still in law school."

"My mother married her company. Cosmetics. She goes to Hong Kong," he said.

"Ever go with her?"

"Back to me again. This is the most lopsided conversation I've ever had," he said and laughed. "Well, if you really want to know," he said, "when I was younger, my mother left me with the housekeeper, Maria, and told her to watch over me. Now my mother asks me to keep on eye on the housekeeper." Even he had to laugh at the thought. But somehow it wasn't really funny.

There were plenty of times I wished my parents would leave me alone. I'd scream and yell at them for interfering in my life, wanting to control every move. Tell me what to do. But somehow, I always knew where they'd be if I really needed them, and the place didn't require a passport to get to or dialing long distance. Just the living room.

"Stop looking at me like that," Nick said uncomfortably,

his hands in his pockets, shaking some loose change.

"Like what?" I asked.

"Like that," he said, pointing to my expression. "Do I look deprived or something?"

"No," I answered, but inside I silently wanted to answer yes. Yes, you do.

A fractured reflection of us rippled in the lake. Our shoulders were almost touching. We looked nice next to each other. Yet Nick appeared much more complicated than I had thought.

I reached into my pocket, took out the snail, and held him in my hand.

"Do you think we're doing him a favor or sending him off to an early frost?"

He took the snail. "Do you think they just die off? Or go to Miami?"

He made me laugh. "You're so practical, Nick. I'm just worried about him."

He looked up reassuringly. "He'll be fine. Set him loose." As he reached out for the snail, our hands accidentally touched. Chills shot across my body and I felt like humming "Two Hearts in Three-Quarter Time." We searched for the right site. A few bushes. A clump of grass and weeds. My concern must have been evident.

Closer to the lake's edge, the soil grew damper, moist, decidedly more luscious. "Perfect," I announced. The snail poked his head out from its shell. "Time to go," I said encouragingly. I put him down and he slowly moved away. He wasn't in a hurry.

"Good-bye," we whispered.

We rose to our feet, brushed the dirt off our clothing, and started off. Halfway out of the park we stopped by a water fountain. A small crack along the cement base allowed water to leak out onto the ground. As we walked away, my muddy sneaker formed a footprint like a waffle iron. Nick grabbed his camera and began shooting my muddy shoe. But I could have sworn that what he was really photographing was me smiling. Things were definitely looking up.

NINE

The rush-hour traffic was building to a peak. Cars were bumper to bumper, and people in buses were packed like sardines. Taxis honked impatiently. But I floated up Broadway obliviously. My hands rubbed against each other where Nick's and my hand had accidently touched.

Before realizing it, I had arrived home. Dinner aromas wafted down the hallway as I floated into the apartment.

Mom called from the kitchen, "Is that you, dear?"

"Yes," I managed to reply in a dreamy voice, then dropped my backpack on the old wooden credenza in the hallway.

"How'd the party go?" Mom asked as I entered the kitchen.

"Interesting," I replied and left it at that, not wanting to change my mood.

A large orange pot bubbled rapidly as Mom chopped the salad. I grabbed a carrot stick. Carrots were a noisy vegetable.

"You're home late today," she said without making me feel guilty.

"I decided to walk home from school."

"Good for your heart." She didn't know how good. She chopped the green peppers into miniature squares.

"Yeah. And it was with this really nice boy." The words had jumped out. I took another bite of carrot.

"Ohh?" Mom's eyebrows arched up. "Does this boy have a name?"

"Nick," I replied, and, as I said his name, it was as if a new person had entered our home. I didn't want to talk about it anymore. She was getting too interested.

"Any calls?" I asked, changing the subject.

"Lauren called. And Carolyn. And Miranda. Boy, it must have been some day."

"It was."

I started for my room, but she stopped me. "Honey. Can't it wait till after dinner? You know what happens once you get on that phone."

I didn't feel like fighting. Not today. Instead, I walked around to set the table, right near her. "Anything you say." She stared at me curiously.

I folded the napkins like the Chinese restaurants do, humming under my breath. Mom watched inquisitively.

When Dad came home, he took off his shoes. I wondered how Nick would have photographed them. Then Dad ritualistically kissed us, looked in the pot, changed his clothes, and took his seat. I took the seat closest to the phone. Richard popped out of his room. He was home for Columbus Day.

Mom began passing the platter. "Veal cutlets. Your favorite." She offered them to me, Richard, and then Dad. She delighted in making us happy. I helped myself to one spoonful of spaghetti. "Is that all you're taking?" Mom asked.

"I think I've had enough spaghetti for one day."

"You had it at school, too?"

"I guess you could say that," I answered.

"Everything you eat shows on you, dear. Look at your shirt."

"Look at her hair. Adri, is that a new style?" Richard teased.

I just smiled awkwardly and tried rubbing some sauce off with my finger; then I passed the spaghetti.

"You're in a strange mood, little Earthlight," Dad observed. "Something special?" He began a mild cross-examination as he chewed.

Richard piped in, "She doesn't need anything special to be in a strange mood, Dad." I know he meant that in a nice way.

"One of those crazy cases you can't talk about?" Mom asked.

"Barbara. Don't tell me you support her wild antics?" Dad said.

Mom looked up at him. "Well, she's not hurting anyone, Charles," she answered.

Richard looked back and forth like a spectator at a tennis match.

"Not according to the guidance counselor." Dad took a sip of wine.

I dropped my fork. "Mrs. Crumper called!"

Mom kept eating. "You know, Adriana, a few weeks ago. With a warning that you better stop those cases of yours."

Richard shot me an empathizing glance as I breathed a sigh of relief. "Hard day at the office, Dad?" Richard asked.

"Don't change the subject." His voice was stern as he wrapped a piece of spaghetti onto his fork. It fell off. Richard and I laughed under our breath.

Just then, the phone rang. I jumped up instinctively.

"Miranda," I answered with a mouth half full. "We're in the middle of dinner. Gotta call you back. Yes; very soon."

"That's not a phone. It's a damn pacifier," Dad commented as I returned to my position.

Richard came to my defense. "Dad, it's the first time the phone has rung all night."

Dad made a sour face. "Well, please don't tie up both lines. I'm expecting a few important business calls."

"No problem." What a grouch, I thought.

"I have a case awaiting arbitration. This client's being sued.

He's been burying people in space, but he's been running into legal problems. They need at least fifteen acres to be officially called a cemetery."

I asked astounded, "You mean bodies are just floating around up there?"

"Zombies!" Richard said.

Mom dropped her fork. "Please, we're eating dinner."

Dad cleared his throat apologetically. "Sorry, darling." Then he wiped the corner of his mouth with his napkin. "So, Adriana, how'd you do on your history exam?"

"Same as in space. We're haaaaaanging in there."

He shot me a look and we all burst into laughter.

"Charles," Mom reasoned, "I think it's good for Adriana to have strong interests. It might get in the way of some grown-ups right now, but it's the traits which she'll need when she grows up."

"I *am* grown up!" I protested, even though she had been coming to my defense.

"Well, you're older, but you're not grown up," Dad interjected.

"But there's nothing wrong with being involved at any age," Mom persisted.

"Some might call Adriana a gossip-monger."

"Not Adriana," Richard chimed in between bites.

"God, Dad! How you could have gone through three years of law school, graduated from New York University—a liberal college—and be so dusty."

Dad leaned toward Adriana. "Come on, where do you think you get this . . . this . . . compulsion to help everyone? Your mother had it long before you did, but kept it in the family."

"Honey." Mom smiled. "That's why I don't want to break her spirit."

"Who's breaking her spirit?" he replied defensively.

"Adriana," Mom said, "you have the right to choose how you want to live your life, and don't ever forget that." With that, Mom seemed to drift very far away. "I wish I had worked a little after college. Instead, I got married and had you kids."

"And then you *really* worked, right, Mom?" Richard said.

"Is that so bad?" Dad asked.

"When I die, I don't want it written on my tombstone: 'Here lies Barbara, she kept a clean house.' "

"Not a chance, Mom." Richard tried lightening the mood.

But Dad was getting riled up. "Barbara, do you find it more fulfilling down there in that soup kitchen?"

"I think she does, Daddy," I volunteered.

"Barbara?"

Mom toyed with her remaining pasta and smiled a very inner, private smile. "You should have seen the face of this nice old lady. I gave her two extra packs of Kraft's cheddar cheese. She was going to save it for her anniversary dinner, but I told her not to nurse it past its expiration date." Then Mom turned to me. "Sometimes you can wait too long to do something." For a moment, she removed herself from the dinner table, from me and Dad and Richard, and drifted off—to places unknown to any of us, perhaps places she might have traveled to if circumstances had been different. That's why I think she didn't want to see me miss my chance. I had to agree with her there. I didn't want to miss my chance either. And I couldn't wait to get it. Just then I realized that I hadn't thought about Nick for ten whole minutes.

When Mom returned to us mentally, she covered up her lapse. "Don't play with your food," she reprimanded me as I twirled a piece of pasta in circles. "You'd think I was serving you escargots instead of your favorite pasta."

"Mom!" I pushed my plate away from me.

She looked at Dad innocently. "What did I say?" she asked. "Did I say something so terrible? Escargot?"

"Don't blame yourself." Dad placed his hands on hers. "She's expressing herself." His voice tried to be calm, but his teeth were clenched.

The thirty-gallon-size Hefty trash bag was filled to capacity, but I made a little more space for my leftovers. "May I please be excused?" I asked, while opening the dishwasher.

"Yes, you may, my sweet," Mom said, recovering. "You must be working on something pretty extraordinary, because I don't understand you at all. Not one bit."

That was all right. Neither did I. I danced into my room and closed the door tightly behind me, then flopped on my bed. They could never understand.

Miranda's phone was busy at first, so I called Carolyn. We had such a long laugh that Mom poked her head in to see if I was all right. "Fine," I said, placing my hand over the receiver and signaling Mom to close the door again. First I gave Carolyn the rundown on my afternoon. Then it was her turn. Dillon had called, fuming. Her off-pitch song had been a violation to their relationship, especially when he had realized she was doing it to get at him, and it had worked. But why, he had asked, didn't she just tell him that she wanted to break up. That's not what she wanted. Only to straighten their wires. Last thing she wanted was a short circuit. But I guess he was still willing to discuss their problems next Saturday night.

When I hung up, I ran to the closet and yanked out a few sweaters and woolen dresses. Under my old set of paints was my shoe box with Carolyn's tapes dating back to prehistoric times. I lay in bed listening to them, then yanked the current one from my backpack and pressed the red Record button.

Boy, all the multiple combinations of rejection that are at your fingertips. Carolyn made a big step today. She declared herself a viable partner. No longer is she willing to live in fear of Dillon not liking her or needing his approval. Today she made a stand. And I think she came out the winner. He doesn't have to like everything she does, but SHE *does. She took a chance. I know I listened to her, so did the other kids. That is, until we became part of one great big salad. I only hope I have the guts to be that strong if and when Nick likes me that much. Nothing like love to test your soul. Only time will tell.*

TEN

Days passed. Each morning my cases and I would meet secretly near the music room on the lower floor. If anyone was in a bad way—anxious, felt left out, or had a bad night—they'd know where to find me so we could talk. The Jefferson button worn upside down was the signal. Carolyn had been wearing hers upside down for one week straight. She and Dillon had been working all week on why they drove each other crazy.

Ellen Levine, another case, felt ugly, no matter what she did. It got so bad that she felt even her own dog ignored her or went howling down the block. One morning Ellen Levine didn't show up for school or come to the underground. Word got out by math that she had been rushed to the hospital in the middle of the night for an emergency appendectomy. Luckily, she was all right. When I visited her in the hospital a few days later, a row of get-well cards were displayed along the windowsill. When I picked them up to look at them, I noticed that different names were signed at the bottom but appeared to be in the same handwriting. Ellen had signed those cards herself! One card read "To my best friend in the world." I placed the card back and tried to cover my awkwardness as I left.

Nick was another matter. The best part of a day was running into him in planned accidents. A glance, a few words were the reward. We'd pause, smile. Soon, it became an obsession.

I couldn't get through the day without having seen him. On Tuesday, when I didn't see him at all, the entire day was wasted. Visits to the girls' room became more frequent, to fix my hair, check the mirror for confirmation. The change in my behavior became apparent.

"What's got into you?" Carolyn quizzed me. But I couldn't stop myself.

Friday afternoon my life made a complete and irreversible three-hundred-sixty-degree turn. Nick asked me to go out for a soda and I immediately said yes!

At Jackson Hole, he devoured a half-pound cheeseburger and french fries while I nursed a cherry coke. "I've been thinking about you."

As we sat there, I noticed Rochelle crossing at Ninety-first Street. Her straight black hair swung along her imported suede jacket. I thought she'd be better suited as a genteel horse trainer or door-to-door alligator salesperson than as a junior at Jefferson. She appeared to be nose-dropping directly into our pane of glass, but the blinding sun turned the glass opaque and she was merely admiring her own reflection. That's what I thought until she came in and sat on the other side of the restaurant. She hadn't noticed us yet.

"Finished?" I tried rushing him.

"Do you have to be somewhere?" he asked.

"No. Not at all," I replied, as we slipped out unseen.

We strolled along Madison Avenue and browsed in a magazine store. They sold cards, too. I bought fourteen birthday cards. "Why do you need so many?" he asked.

"Friends," I replied.

As we walked out of the store, I surprised even myself by pointing out an interesting pair of black high-heeled shoes.

"I want to see what that shoe looks like photographed."

He focused his lens on the three-inch heels. Then he turned to me. "This camera gives reason to everything around me," he confessed, patting it like a pet.

Down the block, a man was selling Sony tapes for a dollar each. An incredible buy. "Here's my reason," I said, holding up three new tapes. That's when Nick asked for my telephone number. I asked for his, too.

Four calls came in a row. Lauren related details of her first rehearsal of *Hamlet*.

"I hope I'm doing the right thing," Lauren said. "I keep getting the feeling something's going to happen."

"That's because you're so happy you're afraid something will spoil it."

Her voice dropped. "Yes, I suppose so."

I hadn't hung up more than a minute when Nellie called. She was a great conversationalist, even when she had nothing to say. Jane called in with a new problem: "A boy's dumping me before we've even spoken. The one on the chess team."

"Want him to notice you? Take the gift wrap off your hair." I thought she took the suggestion well.

By ten-thirty I was exhausted and talked out. I rushed through my math homework, then prepared for bed. Gently I rubbed in Elizabeth Arden Visible Difference cream from the cheekbones out, per Mom's instructions. She said the best time to start taking care of your skin was when you were young. I stared at myself in the mirror. Maybe I was pretty.

The phone rang again, and I dashed into my room. "Hello." I answered breathlessly.

"Hello," I heard back.

"Nick," I answered, surprised.

"I've been trying to reach you all night."

"You have?" Definitely, my phone was placed over consecrated ground.

"I had the operator try. Thought it was out of order," he explained.

"That wasn't what was out of order," I said, unconsciously rubbing the cream in a circle on my cheek.

"Oh . . . ?"

"Well, Lauren's afraid to commit. And Jane's got boyfriend problems. Too many." I laughed.

"Can three hundred and one running shoes pull you away from all that?"

"Sure. But . . . ?"

"The New York Marathon. The spare shoe belongs to a man who's running with a mechanical leg, courtesy of medical engineering. Meet me in front of Rumpelmayer's on Central Park South. Say, eleven in the morning. Is that too early?"

"Early? No, I'm a morning person."

"I'm a night person, but we'll work it out," he said.

I waited for him to hang up, not wanting to break our connection first. When I put down the receiver, my head began to whirl. I floated into my nice warm bed, wrapping the nosegay comforter around my body. It was fluffed up in all the right places. The pillow needed cooling down, though, so I flipped it to the other side. Lauren's tape needed an update. So did Jane's and Carolyn's. But not tonight. That could wait till the morning. Tonight felt different. I wanted to think. I reached over and turned out the little light next to my bed. I wanted this day to last forever, and yet I couldn't wait for tomorrow. But before falling asleep, I felt that the dark seemed just a little less frightening.

ELEVEN

Nothing like a marathon to bring out running shoes. Nick was having a field day in front of Rumplemayer's. I spotted him a block away. Butterflies jumped in my stomach. Nervously I readjusted the rolled-up sleeves on my jean jacket and pulled my hair back. One piece kept falling down, so I tucked it behind my ear.

Nick was just a few yards away. His golden hair shone as if freshly washed. I stuck my feet in front of his camera.

"How about a class running shoe, size six."

He snapped, then looked up. "Got it!" He was in a good mood, with all that assortment of shoes. Pigeon-toed. Open-toed. Name it, he shot it. We crossed over to the park side, with hundreds of other people. Nick glanced down at his watch. "The runners started at the Verrazano Bridge about two hours ago. Some should be crossing the finish line soon. It's eleven–thirty-two and four seconds. Atomic time."

"What time is that? Sounds like it's going to blow up."

"It might," he teased. "Set it at the Smithsonian Institution. Accurate to a thousandth of a second. Me and Big Ben."

I found it interesting that he was so precise. "I never wear a watch," I said. "They seem to stop running. I heard certain people have negative ions that turn a watch off."

He laughed. "I can't see you turning anything off."

"Excuse me." A woman pushed past us. Her T-shirt read:

Who said women can't run the world? She was talking to her friend about the recent Triathlon she ran last summer in England.

"Oh, there's Nellie. Looks like she's coming out of her depression," I said, leading Nick in that direction. But he pulled me back.

"Hey, wait a minute. You said you were off duty."

"Well, you've got your projects, too." I pointed to his camera.

"That's different. It doesn't interfere with people's lives."

"Oh, no? You think pointing that lens at innocent feet isn't stepping on someone's toes?"

"No, I don't. At least I don't pry. I spot it, shoot it, and it's over. Simple."

"So is caring. I spot it, deal with it, and it's over. Simple."

"Come on, Adriana, admit it. You're a bit of a snoop."

"Well, so are you, in your own way." I didn't want to start a fight, but I had to say what I felt.

"Maybe inquisitive," he consented. "All right, maybe you've got something there." He turned his camera toward a sister team of white cowgirl boots with rhinestones. "Okay, okay. You gave me twelve inches and I took a foot," he said. Teasingly, I placed my hands in front of the lens. "You win. Truce," he said, snapping the lens cap back on the camera.

A loud burst of cheers cut our conversation short as the first runners entered the park at Fifty-ninth Street. Four bridges and five boroughs later, it all ended right here.

Television cameras stayed on the first runners as they crossed the finish line. The crowd went wild. The excitement of the crowd pushed us closer together, and I felt his shoulder touching mine. Then officials placed silver foil capes over the drenched and exhausted runners. Our shoulders stayed touching.

"Why are they putting that silver wrap on them?" I asked him.

"Foil acts as a Mylar blanket and keeps the body heat regulated. Prevents hypothermia. A subnormal body heat," he explained matter-of-factly. "But they do look an awful lot like baked potatoes," he added.

Runners came in from Sweden, Canada, Connecticut, Italy, Senegal, North Carolina, Poland, and the Bronx. Seventeen minutes after the first runner appeared, the first women crossed the finish line. Then the oldest runner, Jack Hiller, an accountant from Greenwich Village, who was seventy-nine. Soon Cramie came into view in her turquoise T-shirt, and we applauded her right to the finish line. "She's our librarian," I told some people standing nearby. Nick struck up a conversation with a man next to us as someone eased her way closer.

"Rochelle!" I said.

"That voice. It's like a quiet noise." Rochelle cocked her head like a crow.

"Up to your old oxymorons?" I confronted her.

"Psych it out."

"You're getting to be a real pest, you know that?" I said angrily.

"Rough. Rough. Rough," she answered back, in guttural sounds.

"So that's your problem—you're a dog?"

Then Terri joined us. "Last night, we put your name in an ice cube and froze it," she informed me.

"Old Jamaican voodoo," Jerry jumped in.

"Freezes your soul," Terri added, relishing the prospect.

"Got it from a friend's maid who saw it work. The lady croaked three days later." Rochelle pushed up the sleeves of her angora Italian knit, then curled her black shiny hair around her fingertips.

"Superstition went out with the Ice Age," I sputtered and turned my back.

But Rochelle always got the last word. "Maybe," she warned, "but you'd better have eyes in the back of your head."

"Is anything wrong?" Nick asked.

"Not really. Someone just made a snide remark."

"Don't let it bother you. Whatever they said, it's not true." He smiled as we strolled away from the crowd. Nick picked up an acorn and bent down to lure a squirrel closer.

"Be careful. You can get rabies," I said fearfully. Just then, the squirrel quickly ran up and grabbed the acorn right from his hand, then scampered up an elm tree.

We continued through an arbor leading to Strawberry Fields, named after John Lennon—a lovely manicured section of the park with Japanese trees and a starburst with a single word, *Imagine*. Past that starburst, in the distance, was the boathouse where our snail now lived. I imagined all sorts of possibilities for all of us.

At Seventy-second Street, a girl was crying while her boyfriend watched.

"I think they're breaking up," I projected.

"A-dri-an-a," he accentuated the first and third syllables.

"Okay, okay. I know. No feet. No cases."

"For the rest of the afternoon. That was the deal."

"I'll try harder."

"I can do one better." Nick pulled the camera from his neck and slipped it over mine. "Here." The strap was still warm from his body as it rubbed against my neck. One less thing stood between us now.

"But I have nothing to give you. My tape recorder's at home."

"Oh yes, you do." He reached over and took my hand. Our fingers entwined.

It felt so nice, like opening a hope chest. Where did all these painfully wonderful and unsuspected feelings come from? Had I been carrying them around with me—in my room, on long walks, in quiet corners, everywhere—and never known they existed till now? My mind shut down; something else in me lived. A few minutes passed without a word uttered. And yet, I said more in that short time than in my entire life. Over the park wall, discarded by some marathon runner, lay a silver foil cape. I picked it up. It felt slippery and crinkled to my touch; I placed it around our shoulders. Nick's and mine.

We walked along Columbus Avenue not saying very much, just holding hands, then strolled into a small outdoor café and sat down.

Nick played with his key ring nervously as we waited for the waiter.

"What's that?" I asked.

A sharp-pointed object was looped at the end of his key ring. "A tooth."

"Not yours, I hope."

"From a lion. A Masai warrior gave it to me. Tall as that guy over there." He pointed to a runner. "Dad said I shouldn't exchange money, so we traded instead. I gave the man my belt. My mother traded her blue silk scarf. The Masai lady took her hand-beaded red and white choker right off her neck and handed it to my mother. You should have seen Mom trying on the choker. She said it was her protection against the evil force. The Masai lady just smiled, not understanding a word, and tied the silk scarf around her head."

"And did the Masai warrior put your belt on?"

"The third notch. He was thinner than I was and a mile taller. Dad said that he probably didn't know his own age, but could tell you twenty words for the kind of grass growing nearby and seventy for the color of his cattle."

The waiter brought us menus. We ordered two large Cokes and one chocolate cake with two forks.

"I guess this is our watering hole," I commented, as the waiter walked away. The granite high rises. Downtown, the Chrysler Building. Twin Towers. The day was sparkling clear.

"And those are our foothills of Kilimanjaro," Nick added.

The skyline of New York was ablaze before us and the safari we were on was of an entirely different kind.

"When did you last see your father?" I asked, playing with the napkin at my side.

"The divorce proceedings."

"How long ago was that?" I asked.

"Six years."

"You were ten!" I calculated.

"After the divorce proceedings, he took me to the Big Apple Circus. They were in town at the time." He began playing with his fork, twisting it around a thin groove shaped on the white linen cloth. "During the bear act, who were in pink tutus and turning on a drum, we screamed at the trainer, 'Hey, you're turning them into freaks.' " We both laughed, he more at the memory. Then his expression changed. "How'd we get onto me again?" he muttered in embarrassment. The waiter placed sodas and cake on the table. I couldn't imagine what it was like not seeing your own father for six years.

"Not even a postcard from the San Diego Zoo?" I had to ask. The idea sounded so awful. After all, my parents went off on vacation, but they came back. "You must feel like half an orphan." After I said it, I was sorry. I just blurted it out, but there was no way I could take it back. After that, we didn't say much. My hand reached across the table, between the half-emptied Cokes and crumpled cake. "I can't be your father, but I can be your friend."

This time I picked up the check and left the tip. It didn't come to that much. We started uptown, along the back of the Museum of Natural History. Again, our hands found each other's.

The city was winding down. But one runner was clowning around with her boyfriend, standing on his feet as he walked. Nick yanked the camera off my neck and began clicking away. Then he looked at me sheepishly as I stood shaking my head teasingly.

"All right. All right," he conceded, looking down at his watch. "I made it for two hours, fourteen minutes, and three seconds . . ."

"Atomic time. That's a record."

He gave it some thought. "Actually, it is." He surprised even himself. "Give or take a thousandth of a second."

He smiled. "Tell me more about you," he said.

"Me?"

"That surprise you?" He chuckled.

I paused a moment. "Well . . . my grandparents came over from Poland, and Grandma lived with us. Spent a lot of time with me. My parents met in Brooklyn. They're pretty good most of the time except when they aren't. And I have a brother, Richard, who is three years older than me." I stopped to catch a breath.

Nick stared inquisitively. "Why, Adriana, you've talked about everyone except yourself."

"I have?" I answered, surprised.

"Yes." He was observing me. "Who are you anyway?"

"Adriana," I answered simply, and laughed.

He shook his head. "What am I going to do with you," he said, lightening up the tone.

I slipped my arm through his. "We'll think of something."

TWELVE

They say Sundays are the hardest day of the week. More people get depressed. Maybe it's because Sunday offers promises it usually can't deliver. As for myself, Sundays became a lot more fun. Some Sundays, Nick and I would hang around my house, or we'd take a walk. Go bowling. A museum. A movie. Poke around hardware stores looking at the latest gadgets. It became more and more difficult to be away from him.

One particular Sunday began sagging early in the afternoon. Nick worked on his photos for his contest, so I did my paper for history and couldn't wait to get Nick's reaction. It was called "Chameleon in the Camp," about the survival of prisoners during World War II.

Miranda called and told me she had gotten four more crank calls from a boy with a low, sexy voice who said he was in love with her, and was drawing revealing pictures of her and hanging them over his bed. This was very disturbing to her, and her mother even tried calling the police. Richard, who was packing to head back to school, called a friend's brother who works for the C.I.A., and he said he might be able to arrange to have a tracer put on the calls. Boy, I was glad my brother kept in touch with old friends. Then Nellie's boyfriend wanted exclusivity, but she didn't feel ready to go with just one boy.

Jane was down in the dumps, too. She'd been repeating

I.T.A.T.I. since realizing that the chess boy she really liked wasn't giving her a tumble.

"Why won't he take me seriously?" she asked.

"Look, Jane. Maybe he doesn't like a girl who plays games."

"Well, he plays chess," she replied.

"Those teasing games. Some boys don't like them."

"Really?" She seemed surprised.

"You're constantly making conquests. Number two. Three. One hundred and eight."

"None of them means anything. Except Roger. How do I get him to like me?"

"Maybe you need a map."

"Of what? Cleveland?"

"A map of you. Draw a map. See where you're going. And how you're going to get there without running yourself over."

"Mmm." She thought it over. "A map? I'll try that tomorrow."

"Why not tonight? I mean, if it rains today and you're unhappy, that's okay. But if you're still crying about it ten years from now . . . well . . ."

"All right. All right. I'll do it after the eight o'clock movie."

Lauren sprained her ankle in volleyball. Mickey, from bio, complained about burnout, and a girl in French class was worried her laugh sounded like a laugh track. She's the one who eats eight oranges and wears army fatigues.

The entire tape collection was spread out all over my bed. Then Carolyn called. "I could kill him. This morning he called me a dilettante. That I dabble and don't stick to anything for very long."

"Is it true?"

"No, of course not."

"Would it upset you if he called you a chair?"

She laughed. "NO."

"So maybe it's his problem. Forget it. You're great."

"He's pretty great, too."

"But you're my friend. See you at the deli in the morning. I'm falling asleep."

"This time please come after the chocolate croissant."

"Don't count on it."

"Hey, Adriana . . . thanks for being there."

"You're there for me, aren't you?"

"Yeah." And we both hung up.

I grabbed Carolyn's tape, buried under my comforter with Linda's and Lauren's.

Carolyn and Dillon are still at it, but I guess as long as they're fighting, there's hope. Emotions are a funny thing. It's what we have most of and know the least about. At least Carolyn and Dillon are trying. I guess you'll never get anywhere if you're too afraid of making a mistake. Maybe I'm willing to take that chance, too. For the first time. Maybe I found someone worth taking that chance for. Peek my head out of the shell like our snail, so Nick and I could know each other, really know each other without pretending to be people we're not. Our relationship could be so sweet and good. Stop. It's too scary to even think about it. What if it really happened?

I was late next morning and missed Carolyn. I also missed the morning underground checkup.

Before lunch, I ran down to see Nick. He usually was in the photo lab about this time. It was becoming a habit, meeting each other there a few times a day.

On the side near the enlarger, a man sat alone in the corner, cropping a photo with a mat knife. I hadn't seen him before, but I knew it had to be Mr. Saultern. His white, longish hair was like fallen snow. He was trimming excess tissue paper with

a T square, and nothing distracted his concentration. I stood there and watched him center the print in a mat frame. His roundish face was deeply lined. Mostly, though, as he worked, he exuded a sense of peace. An inner calm. Mellow. Like he had gotten where he was going.

Above the large Formica table where he sat was a row of black-and-white photos blown up and framed along the full length of one wall. An old lady with a babushka tied around her head, clutching a beaten, weathered, empty straw basket. An ancient man, about a hundred years old, standing on a precipice, staring out to the breaking surf, the wind tousling his thinning hair. A couple playing gin rummy on the board-walk at Atlantic City. A lady with a pipe on a rocking chair; a young girl clutching a tattered doll; her brother hugging two cats.

"Hello," I said quietly, moving closer.

He turned around, smiled. "You must be Adriana," he said.

"How'd you know?" I asked.

"Oh," he said, "I have ways." His voice was kind. He took my armload of books. "Here," he said, "let's put your things down." He cleared a place on the tabletop. "Nick'll be back in a jiffy. I sent him for chocolate doughnuts and vanilla soda. Lunch."

"Are these yours?" I walked around the room admiring the blowups, until one held me riveted: a woman in a woven skirt and apron outside a simple saltbox house, staring right into the camera, almost as if she was seeing past the lens. A with-ered twig stuck out from a buttonhole in her blouse.

"You like that one?" he asked. I nodded. "Look at her gaze," he said. "She never bothered anybody. Minded her own business. A quiet, good woman. Worked hard. Calluses on her hands to show it. And as frail as her body was—not

more than a hundred pounds—she had incredible force in that stare." I stood directly under the picture and gazed at it. Her face had dignity. I ran my hand down over my cheek and wondered if I could ever look like that. He continued. "I sent a copy of the photo to her, but she sent it back. Said it scared her. Funny, she couldn't throw it away. She had to send it back. Strange, isn't it? The power of a photo.

"Individuality is a dying breed. The people. The land. I want to see people as free human beings. Free in the sense that their souls can sing out. And not over the hum of a turbine engine." I listened, fascinated. Spellbound. "That's why my work down here is so important. That's why each birthday I give myself a present." His eyes twinkled. "For being allowed to live another year and continue my work. As long as I have birthdays, I'll keep making portraits."

What a lovely celebration, I thought to myself.

"You know," he went on, "a person isn't just going to sit down and tell you their whole life story, but the camera," he said, pointing to the picture, "it's a kind of license. Lets you in."

Now, that license was a much better kind than the one hanging over Mrs. Crumper's desk, I thought.

He shook his head, squinting at his work. "There isn't much call in the world for black-and-white photographs anymore. I make them more for me than for anyone else. So every year, for my birthday, I pick my favorite and blow it up. A present for me."

To give yourself your own unique birthday present was a great idea, I thought.

"When is your birthday?"

"A few more months. January, actually. The twenty-sixth." He placed the mat into a pressing machine, after blowing any

dirt away. He lifted the press and took out the print, then laid it flat on the table to cool, placing a heavy book on top.

The boys in the darkroom left just as Nick appeared carrying a brown paper bag filled with doughnuts and a few cans of soda. I really envied him spending so much of his time down here.

Nick passed around the soda and doughnuts and we laughed and talked. When we had finished, Nick invited me to stay. He had to work on some photos for his entry. Since I had only study hall, I agreed to stay a few minutes. I didn't want to leave him. Not yet.

The smell of chemicals became intoxicating, even pleasant, as Nick adjusted the enlarger. My favorite part was taking blank sheets of paper, shiny side up, and watching an image suddenly appear. He let me do that part.

"Use number six for the maximum zap!" he informed me, handing me the paper.

Mr. Saultern called from the other side of the room. "See you tomorrow, kids."

We were all alone. We continued. Fixer ready. Brush the negative. Turn on the safelight. Focus. He leaned over and I could feel him close to me. My breathing got a little heavy as I tried to concentrate. Focus. Check print. All the while I'm babbling nervously about Carolyn and Dillon and jealousy and Nellie's name change. Is it focused? Is it dark enough? Is the fixer still good? Is it soaking long enough?

He looked so handsome standing there. And I was feeling so nervous. The pull toward him was incredibly strong. Finally we removed the paper with tongs. My hands were shaking as we examined the results. "How's the texture?" I asked.

"A little grainy," he managed to get out. He sounded as if he felt something happening to us, too. His voice was changing—slower, more intense. And the way he was staring into my eyes. "Good shadows and highlights." He indicated them with his finger, then began running his finger along my cheek. My face felt flushed. Nick set the timer and dropped his picture into the fixer solution. I kept chattering about Miranda and *Hamlet* and Lauren as he walked toward the lab door and closed it. Then slowly, he walked toward me. His eyes seemed to ask a question.

"Does it go in the stop solution for sixty seconds? What do you think about Miranda?" I babbled.

"There's only one way to keep you quiet." He came closer.

"How?"

Our lips met for the first time. A part of me fought to hold back—not give into the kiss, afraid of the intensity. I pulled away. A cool breeze ran between us. But then, I couldn't keep away. Being with him seemed the most natural thing in the world. I flung my arms around him, and our lips found each other's again. My heart was pounding. His, too—I could almost hear it thumping. The piercing exhilaration was deliciously painful. Both of us were trembling. Just then, the buzzer went off, but we let it ring a few seconds before pulling apart—enough time for a wildfire to light inside me. Nothing short of a torrential downpour would quench it.

THIRTEEN

Lauren called. She thought her father might have to transfer before the end of the school year. EMERGENCY session. I ran the twelve blocks to her house. Boy, was she in a state. We asked her mother if, in case they had to move, Lauren could stay with me until *Hamlet* was over.

"That's very nice," Mrs. Hartley said, staring at us, "but have you asked your mother?"

"Well, not exactly. First, I thought I'd ask you."

"I'll speak with Mr. Hartley. You speak with your mother. But I don't know. Can't make any promises."

All I could think about as I walked out the door was Lauren's face buried in the *Hamlet* script and tears dropping on the pages.

All the way home I thought to myself, What did I do, encouraging Lauren to do the play? Did I push too far? Maybe I made things harder for her. Not only does she have to leave friends, now there's the play she's totally committed to. God, what did I do?

As soon as I walked in the door, I ran for Lauren's tape.

If Lauren hadn't taken the part of Ophelia, she'd have made the safer choice. But deep down, she really wanted to do this part.

And why should she keep waiting to try for something she really wants? Life will go by waiting. Waiting. Waiting, and then you forget what you were even waiting for. I feel that somehow this is going to work out. But right now I just don't know how.

While we're at it, I'm beginning to feel guilty. Spending more time with Nick than with my cases. If I had given Lauren more time, stayed on top, we might have seen this crisis coming sooner. Might have prevented Lauren's heartache. Maybe my cases are getting shortchanged. But when I'm on the phone with a case and Nick calls, I hurry off to speak to him.

I have to admit that I find myself thinking of other things, too. Like taking out my dusty paint box of acrylics or sketching. The other day I even forgot to turn on the answering machine. What is happening to me?

In late November a frigid cold moved in. Woolen gloves and scarves were scattered around the hallway. Mom suggested inviting Nick for Thanksgiving. He did enjoy spending time around our house, and Mom seemed to love having him since Richard was away at school. Dad, on the other hand, had his reservations. Not because he didn't like him, but he thought I was spending too much time with one person. I told my father I wasn't spending enough.

I nearly forgot. A quick update.

Mom said Lauren could stay with us for a month or so. If it came to that. Mom's a lifesaver. I couldn't wait to tell Lauren the good news at school. The fourteen birthday cards for Ellen were stuffed inside my bag as I dashed out of my building.

When Mom's plane swooped down that morning, it was all wings. The paper had a simple fold and no body, yet was able to fly. I picked it up, fascinated.

Chinese sage says airplane without wings can't fly, but what about wings and no plane?

Wings and no plane. At first the idea seemed absurd. And yet I saw it with my own eyes. Above, Mom smiled. She was watching my reactions. Did she sit up nights perfecting her aerial designs, contemplating my emotional state, keeping a few steps ahead of me?

Carolyn was at the deli as usual, proudly waving a dry cracker. "No salt. No salt," she said. "You happy?"

"Are *you* happy?"

"Do I look happy?" she asked, and I took one step back and looked.

"Be careful, you don't want to get anorexic," I said. "Your button's upside down. What's the matter?"

"Don't ask. Dillon's at it again. Whenever I express myself, he makes that face, like, 'Oh, no, she's at it again.' "

"Maybe that's just his listening face."

"I don't think he likes what he hears."

"Give him a chance."

She bit into her Wasa. "You know, Adriana, maybe Dillon and I are too different."

"Of course you are. You don't want to love a twin." I pulled out my tape recorder as we left the deli.

Eating Wasa under pressure. But all that gaining and losing weight isn't a solution to her problem. The problem's the problem. Maybe we hit it on the head. Maybe they're too different or maybe love is never perfect. Maybe we have to fight for ourselves when we don't even know who that person is yet.

By the time I put the tape recorder back in my pack, we had arrived at school and Carolyn had her checklist out.

"Did you tell it anything interesting?"

"I told it you're on the right track." But she was already checking things off her list. "What are you doing?" I asked her.

"Just let me check one final thing off."

I peeked over her shoulder:

Drink six glasses of water a day.
Speak to Wexler about the Boxer Rebellion.
Have pants taken in at cleaners.
Return books to the library.

"Carolyn! This list is too bo-ring!" I said. "You don't need to plan every minute."

She nodded vigorously. "If I don't keep things in order, they'll fall apart."

"How do you know? Don't plan your life away and forget to live it."

The bell rang for class. I ran up to hang my jacket in my locker. No time to run down and catch Nick before his English literature class.

Unfortunately, Rochelle was late, too. My timing was off. With over four billion people on the planet, why did her locker have to be five down from mine?

"I don't know who picked that outfit for you." She do-si-doed around me.

I smoothed down my jean jumper. "Talking to me?"

"No. Your friend Harvey, the imaginary rabbit." I grabbed my two loose-leaf binders and my American history book for class.

"Don't you think he can see right through you?" she persisted, leaning against my locker door.

"Who, God? The radiologist?"

"Don't you know that Nick is using you?"

"No, I don't. Go back to making ice cubes."

"Well, I know him a lot better than you. Just wait till you bore him to death."

"Sounds like unrequited love to me. Obviously you don't take rejection well."

"Cut your psychological crap. What would he see in schizo girl, anyway?" She flicked her shiny ponytail.

"Twice of what he doesn't see in you." I pushed her aside and slammed my locker closed.

"Why don't you ask him what he did last Sunday night?" She raised her brows.

"Take a burn!" I blurted before turning to go. Richard used that expression and it had always seemed coarse. But it felt pretty good to say it.

I counted the eighteen steps downstairs. I didn't know if Nick would still be in the lab, but I had to see him. Nick was scribbling a note. He didn't see me come up from behind and throw my arms around him. Who cared if the dust was moving? I kissed him on the back of his neck.

"What do I owe this to?" He turned, smiling.

"Rochelle," I blurted out. His expression changed.

"Rochelle?" he repeated.

"Did you two ever go out?"

"Why do you ask?" He pinned the note on the bulletin board.

"So secretive."

"I just don't think I have to give a list, that's all."

"But don't you think I have a right to know?"

"You're just snooping for something. Aren't you?"

"Snooping!" I nearly dropped my binder. "Is it snooping if I want to know if the person I'm going out with is seeing a girl who hates me?"

"Get off my case!" he muttered and walked out of the room.

"I was never on your case." I stormed out.

In the girls' room, I tried collecting myself. Lucy Golden, a real beauty with flowing blond hair and green eyes, had to be combing her hair at that moment. Do you know what it's like to look in the mirror and have a gorgeous creature stare back who's not you? Especially when you just had a fight with your boyfriend? After she walked out, I did the only possible thing—pulled out my tape recorder.

That Rochelle is looking at herself through the wrong end of the microscope. She walks right. Talks right. Dresses right and sure messes things up just right, too. What is her problem?

At lunch, I got Miranda, Carolyn, Jane, and some other girls to sign the birthday cards for Ellen. There were five left, so I signed a few other names, including one from Nick. I had to. We weren't talking because he was giving me the cold shoulder, and I reacted by ignoring him. And I had not invited him over for the holidays. After all, it's hard celebrating Thanksgiving with a person you're not speaking to, even if relatives seem to do it all the time.

Thanksgiving weekend arrived. I only hoped he was as miserable as I was.

The last thing I wanted to do was drown my sorrows in mozzarella, but I'd told the girls I'd go out for pizza. It was the night before Thanksgiving, and they wanted to get me out of my funk. On the way, I mailed the cards to Ellen.

Miranda was a pizza connoisseur. She promised a pizza we'd never forget. First stop was a small pizza joint in the Village, where Miranda boasted they had the thinnest crust. We bought the crust. Next we took off in search of the tangiest sauce. Ray's Pizza on Seventy-second and Columbus was the final stop, where we handed over our nearly completed pizza to a counterman who sprinkled on a generous portion of cheese and a dab of special olive oil before putting it in his oven for us.

This was the most assertive I had ever seen Miranda be as she convinced each pizza parlor to add an ingredient. Today, pizza. Tomorrow, who knows. The possibilities were endless. She was a girl whose time had not yet come.

When the pizza was done, Carolyn had the honor of savoring the first bite. "It's a winner!" she announced. Then, we all dug in.

It was Lauren who first noticed Jane eyeing a boy sitting at the next booth. He was wearing a T-shirt saying *This body climbed Mount Everest.* Carolyn spoke up. "Jane, you got too much sauce on your pizza."

"What am I doing?" Jane asked innocently.

"You know," I said.

"Oh." She shook her head and looked down for the rest of the stay.

"If you're not going to make the climb, don't make the approach," Lauren said to lighten things up.

After finishing every morsel of mozzarella, we got up to leave. All of us agreed that it was definitely one great pizza.

Lauren grabbed my arm. "Let's move. We're being followed."

Mount Everest and friends were after us and gaining. We took off until we lost them. By then, we were at Seventy-ninth Street, along the side of the Museum of Natural History.

Snoopy, Betty Boop, Superman, and other huge balloons were lying flat in the middle of the closed-off street awaiting a dose of helium. Tomorrow morning they'd weave their way downtown toward Macy's in the big Thanksgiving Day parade. A voice called out from the crowd.

"Hey, Greenhorn."

"Mrs. Crumper! What are you doing here?"

"I live nearby. Broadway and Eighty-sixth."

"I'm on Eighty-first."

"See, we have two things in common. Hi, girls," she said, then stared suspiciously. "I hope this isn't a group session."

"No. No," I said, adamantly.

"Good. My husband's here. He's blowing up balloons. Oh, there he is," she said, "blowing up the duck. Must try and get closer."

" 'Bye," we called in unison. Then I turned to Carolyn. "Can you believe my luck? She lives in the neighborhood."

"Don't worry. We don't even know the people who live down the hall."

"Happy Thanksgiving," I said, putting my arms around my friends.

FOURTEEN

Richard was home for Thanksgiving vacation. Mom had made her usual Thanksgiving feast; all the best china and serving plates were out, ready to hold the twenty-five-pound turkey and fixings. After the guests had left, all nineteen of them, Mom and I washed the dishes, Dad closed the table, and Richard ran the vacuum cleaner around the house. I hadn't notice what a well-oiled family we had become after all these years.

Toward evening, Richard sat in his room sorting through some of his papers, squashing them into tight round balls, then tossing them in the wastebasket. Music played in the background. The lyrics of each song reminded me of Nick. I had to admit it, it was the worst Thanksgiving of my life. My heart hadn't been in the turkey or Aunt Faye's trip to Haiti or in all the small talk.

"What are you throwing out?" I peered over Richard's shoulder.

"None of your business." He covered his grades.

"Didn't do so well?"

He just glared at me, so I continued. "Maybe you should save them. In case you want to look them over when you feel less depressed."

His next toss landed in the trash without a rebound. "Listen, little sister, what's good for you isn't necessarily good for me. Get it?" His tone was curt.

With that, I burst into tears. He looked surprised. "Hey, what'd I say?"

"Nothing," I said between sobs. "I'm so miserable." Then I told him about the fight with Nick. "What should I do?"

"You're asking *me* for advice?" He turned, surprised. I nodded through my tears. And he put his arm around me. "I bet he wants to talk as much as you do."

"Do you think so?" I sobbed.

"Why stand on ceremony? Call him."

It was the best call I ever made. Nick had just arrived home from Connecticut. Lots of traffic. Too much food and relatives. And he had been thinking of me all day, too. With only a few words, we made up. "We had our first fight," he said. Then we made a date for the next day.

When he arrived, Mom pulled out the leftovers and warmed up the turkey and sweet potato pie. She was happy to see him, too. The kitchen looked like it had been attacked by aluminum foil. Mom sat down with us and kind of dominated the conversation. I wished she would leave us alone. After dessert, Nick photographed Mom's and my feet under the table. The way we were disagreeing and arguing above the table while our legs crossed and turned identically under the table intrigued him. A mother-daughter study.

Afterward we went to my room. He sat down on my bed as I put on a record.

"Get up," I whispered emphatically. "My father'll have a fit."

"Is this the Freudian couch?" he teased, reclining slightly.

"No, it is not," I whispered louder. "Get up." It was making me nervous to have my parents in the next room. But I must admit I was on the same wavelength. He pulled me down to him. The door was open, but at that moment I didn't care. We kissed. With my parents and brother so close by, I felt especially daring. I suggested we go out for a walk.

We walked uptown along Broadway. The city seemed deserted. People had gone away for the holiday. But I knew one person who was at home. Ellen. As we passed her building, I asked if we could go up for two minutes to wish her a happy birthday. He wasn't keen on the idea, but agreed. Ellen seemed happy to see us and offered us some cake. That's when I noticed the birthday cards lined up on the buffet table. Nick was attracted to all those cards, especially one with a girl in tap shoes. It wasn't until I had talked to Ellen for a few minutes that I realized that Nick was reading the cards with growing suspicion.

"Hey, Adriana . . ." he began, but I hushed him with a smile. He continued reading. Ellen noticed how much attention Nick was giving those cards. She smiled.

"Lot of cards, eh?" He just nodded.

"Come on, Nick, we've got to be going." But he kept looking. That's when he opened the one I signed for him.

"But I didn't . . ."

"Nick, let's go." I grabbed his hand and hurried him out. But it was too late. Ellen's smile disappeared, and she began piecing it all together.

"You sent those cards, didn't you?" she asked. "Didn't you?" Not wanting to believe it.

"Well . . . ," I stammered. "When you sent yourself all those get-well cards . . . I . . ."

"At least I knew who sent them," she lashed back.

"But I thought . . ."

"You thought wrong, Adriana." She glared at me.

I was almost at a loss for words. "Well, it's true . . . that I picked them all. But lots of the kids signed them. I only signed a few."

By now Ellen was fighting back tears. "I see." Nick was

shooting mean glances at me.

"Ellen," I said, "I . . . didn't mean . . ."

"Next time, don't be so helpful," she said softly. "I'd rather get no cards than fifteen from someone who feels sorry for me."

"I'm really sorry," I said. "I really am. I didn't mean to hurt you."

Nick pulled me out of the apartment. "You're impossible," he scolded me. "You just don't know when to stop."

"Maybe I don't," I said. "Maybe I don't."

Monday we returned to school. There was one great thing to look forward to: that week I'd start driver's education. Another was running down to the photo lab at the end of the day. Nick was too busy to talk and nice enough not to bring up the birthday card incident. He had other things on his mind. Mr. Saultern was with him. "We're going over Nick's final photo selection," he explained. "It's got to be in the mail by Thursday." Pictures were strewn everywhere.

"Can I help?" I asked.

"Here." Mr. Saultern handed me a pile of photos. "Have a look. We're down to the last twenty. We only need ten. What do you think?"

Nick shot me a don't-get-involved look, but I took the photos and glanced over them anyway.

"Why, that's my foot. And my mother's!" I squealed in delight. "You mean we've made the semifinals?"

"Yes, you did," Nick said, cutting me off.

"You think you're capturing the outer world in a picture," Mr. Saultern explained, "but what you're getting is an inner world. The best part of a picture." Then he smiled. "I guess I'm always on the job."

"That's okay," Nick chimed in, "so is she."

Funny, but I thought I detected a certain pride in his voice as he said that. We became absorbed in the project at hand. As Mr. Saultern watched us together, I could see by his expression that it brought back memories. "Do you know what is most gratifying . . . watching two people working together. On the same team. Best friends. I had that once with my wife," he said softly.

Nick and I glanced at each other quickly. "A team," I repeated.

Mr. Saultern slipped on his jacket. "Off to a shooting," he told us. We watched him leave.

"He must have been a good husband," I said.

"She must have been a good wife," he replied.

It was getting late, and I had to meet my mother in front of Bloomingdale's to pick out a dress for my cousin Libby's wedding. Nick needed a break, too, so he offered to walk me there. Somewhere between Seventy-fourth and Seventy-third streets, Nick got an idea. "Why don't we collaborate?" He made quotation marks in the air. " 'Footnotes' . . . a column for *The Centurion*. You interview a teacher in depth, and I expose his or her feet. I can even run a come-on picture for the next issue. 'Do you know these feet?' "

My ears perked up at the thought of collaborating. "I like it," I exclaimed. "Let's start with Mr. Saultern."

He shook his head. "I was thinking of someone else."

"Mr. Wexler?" I tried again. But Nick kept shaking his head. "Who, then?" I asked.

He paused. "The Crumper."

"Are you crazy?" I shrieked. "No way, José."

"Meet the enemy head on. It'll be great."

"Then *you* interview her."

"Listen, it might be the best thing to help you two understand each other."

"I don't want to understand her," I said. "You might just as well be sending me off to interview Qadhafi."

"Well, think about it," he said as we approached Bloomingdale's. "She brings you in for meddling, and you meddle with her. In print. It's perfect."

The idea was beginning to sound more appealing. He did have a way of putting things.

"Maybe I should practice on your mother first," I said to him. "She's got to be easier than Crumper."

"You've obviously never met my mother."

"But I'd like to."

"Be careful what you wish. You just might get it."

According to my computations, we'd known each other two months, one week, and three days. And if I really wanted to understand Nick better, it was time to meet the person who'd helped make him the way he was.

After dinner, Nick called. First, he'd mailed off the ten photos for the contest. Mom's and my Thanksgiving feet had made it into the finals. Next the bad news. He had gotten a go-ahead for "Footnotes" from Johnny Johnson, the editor of *The Centurion,* who unfortunately liked the idea of Crumper being the first victim. Complicating matters further, Mrs. Crumper had consented, and Johnny Johnson had set up a time for the interview. One thing, though: he'd failed to mention who was doing the interview.

That night I started my research. At Shakespeare & Company book store, I bought *How to Talk to Practically Anybody about Practically Anything* by Barbara Walters.

Miranda called when I was on Chapter Three. I told her I couldn't talk right then, but she wanted me to know that those annoying phone calls seemed to be stopping. She hadn't gotten any calls that month. I asked her to please withhold any midnight phone calls to me, except emergencies. She said *I* could call *her* any time because she'd probably be tossing around anyway.

FIFTEEN

The morning of the interview, my father was leaving for court. He was trying his outer-space cemetery case that day.

I put on a simple solid blue skirt and navy sweater. I wanted to look inoffensive. My mind was abuzz with hundreds of questions. One tape was securely in place, the other ninety-minute tape stashed in my pocketbook. I was all set—if the interview took place at all.

This morning, the paper plane's message advised, *Have the strength to accept what you can't change and the courage to change what you can.*

I smiled up at Mom and ran the few blocks to the crosstown bus. A slight sense of nausea swept through me.

All through English class, I was kicking myself for allowing Nick to talk me into this. By French, I was positive the world would do very nicely without this article; by biology, I had convinced myself that being a coward was an honorable thing. By Mr. Wexler's class, I was on the brink of packing up my tape recorder and running home.

That's why at one-fifteen, I was actually surprised to find myself standing outside Mrs. Crumper's office. Mrs. Morgenthal, the secretary, pressed her correction button, erasing an entire line of type. I think she made a lot of mistakes. She signaled, "Go right in."

"Think she's human. Think she's human," I kept repeating to myself. My hands turned numb and a sharp pain shot through my right side. Appendix, for sure. I tapped on the door lightly.

"It's open," her voice pierced through the oak lumber. I walked in, and when she looked up from her papers, she screamed in horror, "You! Well, make it quick. I'm about to be interviewed."

"I know. *The Centurion* sent me."

"You!" She sank her head in her hands.

"May I do it?"

She paused. "Dearie. I'm never first around here." She stood over the snailery. "So it's perfect by me."

I pulled out my sharpened pencils, then turned on my tape recorder.

Mrs. Crumper sat down and adjusted her skirt over her legs. "I'll try to be interesting."

"Well"—I cleared my throat—"when did you first realize you wanted to be a guidance counselor and how long did it then take you to achieve your goal?" I asked. A safe question.

She sat up straight and talked carefully, filtering through her thoughts. "If you had asked me yesterday, I'd probably have told you I'm not sure why I ever did go into counseling. Such problems. A kid, whose name I can't mention, thought he'd like to quit school and live for a few years with an archaeologist in central Bali. See what the real world was like. But to answer your question, it took me ten years to get my degree."

"Ten!" I answered, surprised.

"At night. A few credits each semester. Do you know how long that can take? I was teaching during the day."

"Did you know what you wanted to do when you were young?" I asked into the tape recorder, beginning to relax into it.

"Are you kidding? I grew up on the West Side of Manhattan. On a side street. No one in my neighborhood knew what they wanted to be."

"Are you fulfilled in the work you're doing?"

She crossed her legs the other way. "Hey," she said, "shut that thing off a minute." I did. "Listen, I'd quit tomorrow if I could. Would I love taking a sabbatical! But four more years until I get my pension. Why should I give it up? When I retire, you can inherit this office." She laughed.

She made me feel uncomfortable.

"Don't get me wrong. I like my job. But enough is enough. Worked my way through college. I've been working all my life. I want to read a book a day. Travel. Go to Tahiti. Buy a house in Bucks County. Fix up the kitchen."

"Sounds nice."

"Yes. Now I iron my husband's shirts between reading college applications. So kid, enjoy being young. Don't rush. It's over before you blink an eye."

"If you could have done anything, what would it have been?" I asked.

She thought a moment. "A ballerina." She laughed at the thought. I must admit, I did, too.

"Oh, you can turn that thing back on now," she instructed. The Record button got pushed down, the red light glowed. "Next?"

"Are there pressures on you to see that kids get into good colleges?" I read from the second side of my sheet.

Her answer was professional. "I'd say there was too much pressure on kids these days. Academically. To get into good schools. Fun's been taken out of learning. Next."

"Then you think kids feel too much pressure for college."

"Absolutely," she answered, then waved her hand in the air. "Turn that thing off again." And she turned to me. "*Entre nous,* this is good. Very good. At least now you're asking questions that aren't going to get you into trouble. Right, kid?" I just smiled. "Right. You might even make it out of school. Next month is reevaluation. I'll have to remember this."

Perhaps Nick was right about this interview, I thought to myself. "Can I turn the tape back on?" I asked, wanting to get back to the interview.

"If you insist," she replied.

"Mrs. Crumper, what qualities are important in being a guidance counselor?" I asked, returning to my official interviewer's voice.

"Not yours." She laughed robustly. "First," her tone growing more serious, "you should be grown up. Yes. And mature, with a degree. That helps. Not baby fur behind your ears." She leaned over and peeked behind mine.

"I'm not a baby, if that's what you're implying."

"You're not grown up either, Miss Greenhorn, if that's what you're thinking."

"That's a matter of opinion," I answered sharply.

"Exactly. And I get paid for mine. And I'd say you'll be mature when you realize you're not the center of the universe."

"I never thought I was," I stammered, adjusting the volume button and putting in a new tape. "Getting back to you, Mrs. Crumper, it's been said your strong suit is getting kids into crackerjack schools."

"Meaning . . . ?"

"Meaning you know your colleges."

"And I don't know my kids?"

"I didn't say that." This interview was falling apart, and I desperately wanted to salvage what we had left.

"Stop here. I think you're saying something else. Implying something."

"No, I wasn't," I answered, flustered.

"You're not in here to interview me. Are you? You're here to prove something."

My mouth dropped open. "That's not true. I really want to interview you."

"Why?" she asked.

"Because I thought maybe we could understand each other better." There was an element of truth to that. A little, anyway.

"Go find someone else for your article."

I sat there shocked. "I'm sorry, Mrs. Crumper. I didn't mean to offend you."

She turned around, glaring. "Shut that damn thing off, or I'll throw it in the trash. You and that . . . that tape recorder of yours!"

"Mrs. Crumper, I think what you said was very interesting. Do you think we can use the beginning part? Or some of the middle? People would be interested in what you have to say." She didn't answer. "Can you give me something positive to end the article with?"

She stood up solemnly and remained there for what seemed like an interminable period, then stared right at me. "You want something positive? I'll give it to you. Interview yourself," she said. "That's my advice for the day."

I didn't stop running until I reached the lobby. Jane hadn't seen Nick. Gloria thought she heard him say he was going to the hamburger joint. I ran around the block and opened the door. Sitting in the corner were Nick and Rochelle, deeply engaged in conversation. It was like watching a silent film turn into *Friday the Thirteenth, Part Six*. They didn't see me. Rochelle was glued to Nick's every word. At various points she laughed so hard it made me wonder what he could be saying that was so hilarious. From my vantage point, there was nothing funny. Some team we had.

I waited at the corner, inside the bakery. After fifteen minutes, the French lady kept eyeing me suspiciously.

Maybe Lauren was right. It was better not to get involved. Then I saw them. They left together, but Rochelle turned downtown while Nick turned toward school. As he passed the bakery, I jumped out. "How could you do that," I screamed. "How could you do that!"

He jumped. "Hey, wait a minute," he said, taking my hands, trying to calm me. But I pulled away.

"Nothing would make her happier than to come between us."

He stood there calmly. "You're overreacting, aren't you? All I did was have a soda with her."

"French fries, too. With a person who hates me."

"You're making this into more than it is. Rochelle and I are friends. That's all."

"That's what you think. You're so gullible!"

"Adriana."

"How do you think I feel?" I asked him.

"Jealous," he said, smiling and putting his arm around me. "But it's you I care about, not her."

"Well, you have a funny way of showing it."

"Can't I even have a drink with someone? She wanted to ask me about a problem she was having."

"Since when are you interested in other people's personal problems?"

"Advice about her TV show."

"Believe me, she'll make it personal." We stood there silently. "While I'm in there being barbecued, you're out here collaborating with the enemy." I burst into tears.

"I guess the interview didn't go well," he said compassionately.

"It went terribly. Awful. I asked all the wrong questions."

"Maybe it went better than you thought."

I shook my head. "I have the tape to prove it. Crumper thought I should interview myself instead. Can you believe that? And when I ran to tell you, you're here with her."

His tone changed and he smiled. "Are we still a team?" he asked, handing me a tissue. I just stared at him. I wanted to say yes, but it still hurt. "You get all worked up. Like with your cases. You just take everything to heart."

"I can't help it," I answered. "I don't know any other way to take it! And don't try to change me, Nick Buckley. Not you. Or Crumper. Or anybody." I turned and ran down the now-deserted street.

"Adriana, wait," he called. But by now I was past the corner, running as far away as my legs could take me, and when they ran out, I took the bus.

All Mom had to do was look at my face. "Honey, it's only an interview. Not the end of the world."

She held me close like she did when I was little. It felt good at any age, and she held me for a long time. The phone rang but we didn't answer it. She just stayed with me like when I had chicken pox.

"Mom," I finally said.

"Yes," she answered, "I'm still here."

"I'm glad."

"Me, too." Then she said softly, "You are the joy of my life."

"I am?" I asked.

She tousled my hair. "You always are. Always will be." We talked, until we realized our faces were in shadow. It was getting dark.

"Where'd the day go?" she said.

"Good riddance," I said, watching her turn on the little light next to my bed.

Her face was soft, almost incandescent in the lamp's glow. I wanted never to see Mom grow old. I wanted her to stay this way forever.

When Dad came home, he walked into my room and kissed us. Mom first. "I won my case," he proudly boasted. "The cemetery plots are still on hold." We burst into hysterics.

"See," Mom said, "as long as you can laugh, there'll be another day."

While I was transcribing Crumper's tape, Lauren called. Her mother thought it would be all right for her to stay at my house, if it came to that. But her father wouldn't comment until he knew all the facts. Didn't sound like a magazine reporter to me.

Lauren is getting scared, very anxious. Can't concentrate on homework. How can she constantly leave everything behind, let go of what she cares about? How can I? Jealousy can be dangerous. And scary. I think I'm beginning to need him more than he needs me. What if Nick decided to move away in a different way? What if I'm alone again?

Finally, around ten, I got off the phone with my cases and returned to transcribing Crumper's tapes. I was determined to make something out of that interview. The phone rang in the middle of a sentence. "Hello," I answered, turning off the typewriter.

"Hello . . ." I heard a hesitant voice.

"Nick?"

"Are you there?" he asked.

I paused. "Yes."

"I'm sorry about today. That I upset you." I didn't respond. "Do you forgive me?" he asked.

I felt him embracing me through the wires. I paused. "Yes," I said, "of course I do. Oh, Nick, do you know the Crumper's crushed in her job? She's so unhappy. I felt sorry for her. Wait till she reads the article. Oh, Nick, something's missing from her life, and it scares me. I don't want it missing from mine."

"What are you afraid of missing?" he asked.

"Why, Nick," I replied, beaming from ear to ear, "you're asking me questions. You're getting analytic."

"I guess I am," he admitted.

"But you can't take a picture of it," I teased happily.

"I love you," he said almost audibly.

"I love you, too," I answered. I didn't even need to think.

Amazing how a day can make a three-hundred-and-sixty degree turn. Within less than twelve hours, I had cried more than in my whole life and yet I never felt more wonderful. Whatever was happening to me, I was beginning to like it.

SIXTEEN

After turning in my article for the newspaper, I ran to the cafeteria to meet Carolyn and Dillon. Nick joined us from another table. It was Hungarian goulash day. International Food Week at school left us pretty hungry.

Just then, Rochelle's face beamed across the closed-circuit TV waves with her weekly update. Her friends, Terri and Jerry, turned the volume up. I dropped my fork. Nick laughed, but watching Rochelle made me nervous.

"Our Chistmas/Winter Solstice assembly will be held next Friday. Dr. Martham wants to remind everyone to elect their class representative for the candle lighting ceremony. Musical students with jazz problems, please see the librarian. *Hamlet* people with fencing problems, see Mr. Wexler." I watched Nick listen.

That evening was a heavy phone night. Little time to study for a math test. Carolyn thought her relationship might be making a breakthrough. A whole week without a fight. Miranda called. Alex, the kettledrum boy, had asked her to practice "Rhapsody in Blue" with him. Jane hadn't had a date in over three weeks. She was waiting for Mr. Chess.

I could tell when Lauren called that something was very wrong. My heart dropped. "You're leaving, aren't you?" I just knew. She was silent, then her voice quivered, "Yes."

"Oh, no."

"In the spring. A month before *Hamlet* opens."

Lauren sat at the other end and couldn't even speak. She sounded lost.

"Wait. I'll be right over."

I dropped my paper contrasting Gilgamesh, the Sumerian superhero, and the Netsilik Eskimos, grabbed some money I'd stashed away, and hopped in a cab headed for Lauren's house. Her father was at a desk in the corner, going over papers.

"Mr. Hartley," I said, going over to him, "Lauren's put her heart into doing the part of Ophelia."

"I know that," he said. "Moving is hard."

"Excuse me, but did you know that she was afraid to take the part because she thought she might never get a chance to play it? Do you know what a risk she took? It would have been easier not to try. It was hard for her to say yes. And do you know how good she is? I've peeked in. You'd be so proud, I know it. Please, Mr. Hartley, please, can't she stay until the play's over? Can't some things be as important as a career? I mean, I know this is your job, but Lauren needs something too, something that can't be taken from her."

He listened, then looked at Lauren. "This play is that important to you, Lauren?"

"Yes, Daddy, it is."

He appeared to be mulling it over. "Mmm," he said. "You did make a commitment. Oh, honey, I didn't realize how hard it is on you. All that changing. You used to like it. Traveling. Meeting new people. But you have a life of your own now." Then he turned to me. "I'll think about it," he said. "I will." Lauren ran into his arms, and hugged him just for the possibilities.

When I returned home, Nick called. His mother was leaving for Hong Kong next week and wanted to meet me before she left. Would I come for dinner on Thursday?

"What if she doesn't like me?"

"That's okay. She doesn't like me either."

"Oh, Nick, you have such a twisted sense of humor."

When I hung up, I sat in bed for a long time daydreaming. There was so much about Nick I wanted to know. There was something I couldn't put my finger on, like a part missing from a puzzle. Meeting his mother might help.

The day before the dinner, Carolyn came over to study. My room was a disaster area. Blouses were tossed all over the floor. A blue blazer—too straight. Pants—too casual. A rejected bugle-beaded sweater dress—too flashy. My wardrobe was appalling. Everything seemed old and wrong. Everything I tried on made me look ugly and fat. Nothing was *me* anymore. Carolyn left, I threw the whole mess into the closet.

Thursday night, I slipped on a wine-colored skirt and paisley silk blouse. Then I couldn't find the black belt with the silver buckle. Even more, I needed by other black shoe. I don't know why I always seem to lose my clothes in the closet. Next week, I said, it's going out, all of it.

"Time to go," Mom called from the other room.

I panicked. On my hands and knees, I squirreled through the mess and found it, quite unexpectedly, in an old box of freshman art projects.

"Well, you look very nice," Mom said, as I slipped the other shoe on. "Tuck the shirt in."

"Mom, you're so old-fashioned." I grabbed my watch and sprayed half of her Chloe perfume all over me. I was totally discombobulated as I ran out the door. A cab was in front of the building and I jumped in.

SEVENTEEN

The doorman signaled me up. In the chrome reflection in the elevator I saw that my hair had gone haywire. My hands were shaking, and, I'd forgotten to polish my nails. His mother was a stickler for hands.

Nick answered the door. The last thing he whispered before we went into the living room was, "You're going to hate her."

A tall, stately blond lady extended her hand. "Hello, Adriana. I'm Mrs. Buckley. Sally Buckley."

Her smile helped put me at ease. She was taller than I expected. About five eight. And she had more grace and elegance than the usual mom. Her skin was very white, delicate, like Dresden china, and you could almost see blue veins running underneath. She was polished to a high gloss.

The living room reminded me of an English country house, not a co-op in the middle of New York City. There was antique furniture and colorful objets d'art, many Oriental in design, in glass cases.

"It's all so beautiful." I gazed in awe.

Mrs. Buckley seemed pleased. "You like it?"

Nick shot me a look. He was mixing us drinks at the bar. "Orangina okay?" I nodded. He looked so handsome there in his light blue shirt, sleeves rolled up, not at all like the times he'd be mixing chemical hydroquinone solutions. He seemed relaxed, but a little more reserved.

I took a bite of the hors d'oeuvre she offered. "Shrimp?" I asked. Carolyn would have gone crazy here.

"Yes," she answered, watching me stare around. "I collect these things on my travels," she explained.

"Boy, you must do some traveling." My eyes darted from one thing to the next. Two blue-and-white songbirds danced on a fruit tree, ducks sat in the middle of an octagonal dish. There were ceramic vases with short necks and long necks.

"Very rare," she explained about a figure of a horse. "Sung dynasty." We continued around the room. "Here's one of my favorites," she said, as Nick handed us our drinks. It was of a child sitting on a stool. "Ming dynasty. I bought it when Nick was about that age." The young figure held a lantern with a sea creature. "A flying carp. Nick loved fishing as a child."

"Boy," I said, impressed.

"One day, Nick had a friend over, Billy Minton. Remember, Nicky?" She turned to him. "Whoops. He doesn't like me to call him that." She corrected herself. "Nick. Anyway, Billy was on the clumsy side."

"Well, you made him a nervous wreck, the way you kept following him around."

"Who wouldn't be? One time he broke a seventeenth-century tureen," she told me.

"Mom, living here's an occupational hazard."

"You talk like you can't have friends up."

"Well, you're not crazy about the idea."

"Sometimes a bunch of kids can get pretty rowdy," she explained to me.

"Come here," she said, "I've saved the best for last." We walked through a hallway filled with clocks. A turtle clock. A

pearl clock. Even a grandfather clock. Then, we stopped at the most dazzling of all.

"My mom's favorite," Nick said.

"A chimera mystery clock. Priceless." Mrs. Buckley feasted her eyes.

"A mystery clock?" I leaned over for a closer inspection. "Why?"

"It is impossible to understand how it operates," she explained. "The secret is guarded by the sphinx herself. Rumor had it that it was once owned by a maharaja . . . if you can believe that."

"I can!"

"Trevor and I bought it . . . I mean, Nick's father and I bought it to celebrate Nick's birth." That was the first time she had mentioned Nick's father. "Nick used to watch the hours pass. Remember, darling? When Nick learned to talk, he'd ask, 'Where's the mera?' "

"Mom! I don't think she's interested." He tried to stop her.

"Oh, I am." I wanted to hear more.

"That's why I call the clock my 'Flight of Time,' because I watched Nick grow with that clock."

"Mom, the clock stopped working years ago."

"That's part of the mystery," she said and laughed.

I put my hand over the smooth onyx and jade. The two hands were suspended in the middle of the piece without any apparent connection to the movement.

"I've got the answer worked out," Nick said.

"I don't think so, honey. The only one who knows is Cartier's. They made only ninety of them and they're not talking."

"Well, I think it works on a double axle system with pendulous dials."

"Just like him to need to figure it out. I like to think it runs

on moonbeams and let it remain a mystery forever. Nick's got to bring in axles." She put her hand on his shoulder. "Leave some things to the imagination, sweetheart." Then she turned to me. "He's so practical."

I couldn't take my eyes off that clock.

"Dinner." A maid in a starched white uniform popped in from the kitchen.

"Thank you, Maria." Mrs. Buckley showed us to our seats. The table was set with beautiful dishes, long-stem glasses, and elegantly folded napkins. Far above the usual fare for Thursday dinner around our house, or Saturday or Sunday for that matter.

"Smells good." I inhaled delicious aromas—but what if I used the wrong fork? What if they brought out wild boar? Baby eel sizzling in oil?

During the appetizer, a white-looking soup she called vichyssoise, Mrs. Buckley talked about reversing the aging process by returning elasticity to the face. Then she wanted to know about me. "Adriana's an unusual name," she said, fishing.

"My parents conceived me on a cruise near Venice. Somewhere on the Adriatic Sea."

"Are you sure you weren't named after Adriana Le-Couvre?"

"Who's she?"

"A famous actress of the sixteenth century, Voltaire's mistress."

"No." I laughed from embarrassment.

"They made an opera out of the story. She loved violets."

"I love violets."

"But she was poisoned by them."

"Oh," I said, dropping my spoon in the soup.

"Adriana's heavy into therapy." Nick changed the subject.

"Oh," she said, like she felt sorry for me, "you're in analysis?"

"No, Mom," he explained, "she's the doctor."

"See, Mrs. Buckley, people come to me for help."

"Help! Help for what?" she asked, astounded.

"Your typical breakdown. Approach-avoidance. Burnout. Mini-traumas. That kind of thing," I explained.

"Mom, she's planning on saving the world."

I smiled embarrassedly, because I didn't think she understood. Actually, Nick seemed proud of me.

Mrs. Buckley looked slightly horrified. "That's cute," she said.

"I have about fifteen cases. Depending on the season, Christmas being the busiest. Lots of depression. Summer slows down a bit—lots of kids are away."

"Adolescents," she said shaking her head. Then, she noticed me making a face. "You don't like that term?"

"Well, it sounds like we're not people. It's like calling little kids tots," I said.

Nick laughed. "Calling us names isn't going to help, Mom."

Mrs. Buckley seemed relieved when Maria brought out the ham. She changed the subject to something safer. "Are you in Nick's nineteenth-century literature class?"

"Mom. That was last year."

"Oh." She covered her embarrassment. "Now it's Byron? Shelley? I have a book I promised you in my room."

Nick interrupted. "We had a test on that unit last week."

"I must have been away," she explained, cutting a piece of ham.

Then the phone rang and Maria poked her head in. "For you, Mrs. Buckley." She got up from the table.

"Excuse me."

"Hong Kong calling," Nick said snidely.

I leaned across the ham. "She's not so bad."

"That's because she's not your mother."

"I think she's interesting."

"Want to take her home with the leftovers?" he teased.

"No, thanks. One mother to a customer."

He reached over and took my hand under the table, and we stared at each other until Mrs. Buckley returned.

"They're having trouble mixing a few dye lots. Cobalt blue and ginger red," she told me.

"You must spend a lot of time in Hong Kong," I said.

"She's thinking of applying for dual citizenship," Nick chimed in.

"It *does* give us a life we want."

"Mom. I like chicken. Eighty-nine cents a pound."

"You like cameras, too."

"I can use only one at a time." There was a painful silence. I thought about the ceramics and the young boy with the lantern and the chimera clock and couldn't help but wonder why her feelings toward her son were best expressed in inanimate objects.

Maria started clearing the table. "My one luxury," Mrs. Buckley said. The rule of thumb around our house was "Do unto yourself as you would like others to do unto you." But I didn't tell her that.

After dinner, Nick played the piano. A polonaise. I hadn't known he could play the piano. Then he wanted to show me his room. We were happy to finally be alone.

His room was filled to capacity with stereo equipment, electronic typewriter, IBM computer, and lots of books on photography. No wonder his mother had to go to Hong Kong and work so hard to afford all this. A small stuffed bear served as librarian on the bookshelf. But the best was his bathroom. There were cages all over. An iguana, Gila monster, baby fox, all living side by side. He took out a brown ferret and let me pet it for a while. It felt so soft and cuddled in my hand. "He's so cute."

Across from his bed were a few photos in silver frames. I picked one up with my free hand; in the other I hugged the ferret.

"Is that your father?" I asked.

He nodded.

"You look like him. The eyes and the smile."

He laughed briefly, then seemed very far away.

"You look happy together," I commented.

His father had a strong presence, even dressed in a simple khaki shirt. He had his arm around his son and his eyes reflected pride. When I placed the photo back on the shelf, Nick said nothing. Nobody says very much about him, I thought. "Do you miss him a lot?"

"I think it's getting late," Nick interjected. Obviously that topic was off limits.

"Oh, yes," I said, looking down at my watch. It was a half hour later than I said I'd be home. "Can I call home before I go?"

He directed me into the den, then returned to his room. I had started to dial when I noticed a pale pink lacy phone book on a small telephone table. I flipped through it as I waited for Mom to answer. I turned to A. Then B. Buckley. Lots of Buckleys. Uncle Harry. Aunt Lynn. Then Trevor. I slammed the book closed. Mom answered. I said I was on my way. The pink lacy book was sitting there. No one was nearby. Quickly, I opened the book to B, darted down the page to Trevor. A number in New Jersey. I recognized the 201 area code. That had to be him: 271-7318. I repeated the number to myself over and over again. No pencil was available, so I committed it to memory as I slammed the book closed.

Twenty-seven was Mom's birth date. Seventeen was my age, almost. Three was Dad's lucky number, and Richard had eighteen on the back of his old soccer shirt.

"Everything all right?" Nick asked, coming in. He brought my coat.

"I really had a good time," I said.

After thanking Mrs. Buckley, I walked to the elevator with Nick. "Isn't she a lulu?" he said.

"Oh, she's not all that bad." But my mind was on my mother's birthday and my father's lucky number.

"I think she's nicer to strangers."

"Nick. I think she loves you very much."

"I must have missed that part. Somewhere between the ham and dessert."

"Between the lines, silly," I added. "The boy fishing. The clock. Your birth was a celebration."

We were in front of his building now, and it was freezing. Nick was in his shirt-sleeves.

"Go in. You'll catch cold," I urged him, still repeating the numbers in my mind.

"What are you mumbling?"

"Nothing," I lied. "My teeth are chattering."

"They chatter even when you're not talking," he teased, leaning over and giving me a kiss.

"Your teeth are chattering, too."

He gave me another wintry kiss, then put me in a cab. "Go in," I begged, as he closed the taxi door.

I asked the driver for a pencil. Instead, he began telling me his life story about coming here from Russia two years ago with his wife and three-year-old daughter. My mind drifted, but soon returned to my mother's birthday. My father's lucky number. My brother's what? Oh, no. I couldn't remember. My brother's what?

When I arrived home, my mother was dozing off, but Dad called me in to say good-night. I was too tired to tell him all that had happened.

I ran to my room, closed the door, and wrote down what I remembered of my mother's birthday and Dad's lucky number.

I paced, but couldn't relax, much less sleep. I thought about Nick. I kept thinking about his mother in Hong Kong. Her not even knowing what Nick was studying. The friction between them. The photograph of his father near his bed. The emptiness whenever his father was mentioned. The sadness in his eyes.

I pulled a shoe box out of my closet. Then I yanked a fresh tape from my drawer and tore open the plastic wrapping. Quickly I grabbed a pen from my top drawer and wrote neatly across the tape in my best handwriting, *Nick Buckley*. I dictated well into the night.

EIGHTEEN

"Footnotes" came out the following Tuesday. After third period, Johnny Johnson and his staff distributed the paper. In the lobby, I grabbed the first copy I could. There it was, on page six. My name. Well, Adriana Earthlight, that's the name I used, a nom de plume. And Nick Buckley. Side by side. I watched from behind a pillar as kids took copies. Some skimmed or just read the headlines. Gloria stayed on page six with a poker face, Tim and a few boys chuckled. My tongue was hanging out for feedback. I had a full-blown case of paranoia. Finally, Miranda said the article made her feel a little sad, and Lauren mentioned that Mrs. Crumper must do a lot of ironing and underneath feel she had missed her chance. Carolyn was very proud of me. And Bobby Stevens and Lynn Dunlapp suggested themselves for the next interview. No one had warned me that writing would be so painful.

Last period, Mrs. Crumper came dashing through the hall. "Hey, Greenhorn," she called out. "I'm off to a symposium on snoring . . . want to come?" she teased.

My heart stopped. "Did you see the article?"

"Got one on my desk and the other stuffed in my panty-hose."

"Then you liked it?"

"Liked it? I didn't say half those things! Ironing shirts. Trips to Tahiti. Wanting to clear out."

"But you did, really!"

She didn't like that. "Next issue, I hope it's *your* feet plastered at the bottom of that article!"

"But, Mrs. Crumper, people like the article. Feel they know you better."

"Better than what? Still, all things being equal, stick to the written word."

Carolyn found me standing there with my mouth open. "What's the verdict?"

"She's still on my case." Then I took a double take. "Carolyn, you cut your hair!" Her long hair was stylishly cut to her ears.

"Like it?" she asked, patting down the short ends.

"Very pretty. Yes," I smiled.

"Dillon had a fit. Do you think it was wrong to get my hair cut without asking him first?"

"Of course not. It's your hair. Do you like it?"

"I do. But he hates it."

"Tell him each to his own taste."

"Yeah, otherwise it's like his ordering my dinner." With food on her mind, Carolyn invited me to come over for dinner Friday, then go to a movie. We hadn't done that in a long time.

After Carolyn left, I pulled out my tape recorder.

Carolyn is still struggling in this relationship. But there must be something very strong between them if they're still working at it. She also hasn't stopped fighting for herself. Maybe that's the only way they can really have a good relationship, eventually. I wonder if I change around Nick, too. Does he really know who I am? Would he still like me if he did? Would I? Whom am I, anyway?

Next day in library, Nick and I were planning the next "Footnotes." But whose feet would be in the next issue? I wanted

Mr. Saultern, but he thought Cramie. He suggested we fight it out at his house on Friday night. "My mother's in Hong Kong." He smiled evilly.

"But your mother doesn't like anyone up when she's not home."

"She's checked your agility, and you passed with flying colors."

"Only because it was a good night." I laughed at my own tendency to large movements. "And I've already made plans with Carolyn for Friday night. We're seeing a movie."

"Great. Ask Carolyn and Dillon to come, too." He slammed his book shut. "Off to physics. We're on for Friday. Remember, it's the winter solstice. The shortest day of the year, so we've got to work fast," he teased. I didn't have a chance to say no, even if I'd wanted to.

As I left, I saw Rochelle lingering around the biography section of the stacks, on the other side of where we had been standing. She tried to act inconspicuous, but she looked a little too nonchalant.

Carolyn and Dillon accepted Nick's invitation and the next few days Carolyn and I spent on our winter solstice outfit. *Vogue* and *Seventeen* magazines didn't cover the appropriate "solstice" look, so we were on our own. I really wanted to make the most of the short time we'd have together, romantically speaking. Whenever I closed my eyes, I saw Nick and me alone, with low music and candlelight.

I told Mom I was going to Nick's with Carolyn and Dillon, but left out one bit of information: his mother was in Hong Kong and Maria would be off. For me, that was the most exciting part of the evening, but I thought my mother would have another opinion. I put on a soft pink shirt and flowered skirt and let my hair hang loosely over my shoulders. Nick liked my hair that way.

Carolyn and Dillon met me at Seventy-second and Columbus and we walked to the crosstown bus together.

"Come on, you girls, stop cackling," Dillon said.

"Next time he says that, I'm going to scream," Carolyn told
me. When he said it again, Carolyn screamed.

"Okay, you asked for it," Dillon said, picking Carolyn up
over his shoulder in a fireman's carry and running down the
street with her.

Carolyn screamed again—in protest. "Put me down. Put
me down, you brute! Or I'll . . . I'll tell you what's on my
mind!"

He deposited her back on the ground. "Anything but that,"
he begged.

"Come on, tell Adriana you like a girl who's more of a
challenge." Carolyn egged him on.

"You said it, I didn't." He hopped on the bus after us.

Before Dillon got to the back of the bus, Carolyn turned
to me. "Isn't it crazy? I want to keep this relationship going
and change it at the same time."

Dillon sat there laughing and talking with his usual joie de
vivre. I watched them together. His arm was around the back
of the blue plastic seat, and, despite their differences, I hoped
they'd work it out. Mom had told me once that even married
people grow at different rates. One can grow a few years ahead
while the other stays in the same place. So one partner waits
for the other to catch up. Some never do. And sometimes a
person doesn't wait. Sometimes they get divorced. All I hoped
was that Nick and I would grow at nearly the same pace, and
in the same place. Some sharpened pencils in my pocketbook
jabbed into my ribs and I wondered if we'd get to "Footnotes"
at all that night.

NINETEEN

The apartment was empty. Just us and a few hundred pieces of ceramic and priceless antiques. Nick made us drinks while I gave Dillon and Carolyn a crash course in Ming and Sung dynasties. Then we stood in front of the chimera clock. "Be careful of that," I warned. "It's priceless."

"Don't worry about me," Dillon said. "I've got on my best antique behavior." Carolyn pushed him affectionately.

By the time we returned to the kitchen, Nick had half the contents of the refrigerator pulled out. Obviously, Maria had prepared a few things for him before leaving for the weekend. Nick was cutting into a foot-long hero loaf and we helped stuff it with ham, cheese, olives, and a layer of tomato. Nick took command of the kitchen as if he enjoyed it. Carolyn pulled out the glasses, and I set the table. Very domestic, the four of us. Before we sat down at the kitchen table, Nick dimmed the lights. But before we took our first bite, the bell rang.

We weren't expecting anybody. Nick went to the door.

"Lynn Van Der Camp. Jimmy," he said, startled.

"Well, aren't you going to invite us in?" Lynn asked. Carolyn's eyes darted toward mine.

"What's she doing here?"

"Don't look at me," I answered.

No sooner had Lynn and Jimmy entered the kitchen, and I had offered them some hero sandwich, than the bell rang again. This time it was a few kids that Nick knew from the photo lab, with three girls from another school. Nick seemed confused, but graciously offered them a sandwich. The large hero was soon gone.

Then Miranda arrived with the kettledrum boy. And Jane and the chess player, among others. Now there were about twenty kids in the apartment. I ran up to Jane. "What are you doing here?" I asked, pulling her aside.

"Café Mom's Away," Jane said.

"Café Mom's Away?"

"Yes. His mom's away, isn't she?"

"Well, yes . . ."

"So when parents are away for the weekend, the news hits the phone chain."

"Phone chain . . . but how did you know his mother's away?" I asked her.

"Came over the airwaves this afternoon. Café Mom's Away at Nick Buckley's house tonight."

"Who would know . . .?" I started to say, and Jane rolled her eyes toward someone across the room.

"Rochelle!" I exclaimed. "Boy, that's trouble." She stood there grinning next to Louis the Ape.

"On her TV program. Then I got a call, too." Jane explained. "I didn't call you because I thought you knew." Just then seven more people arrived, carrying bottles of wine under their arms.

"Is this the winter solstice party?" one of them asked.

"Café Mom's Away," Rochelle greeted them at the door.

I couldn't believe it. I thought I had had a hotline for years, but I must have been on another circuit. I thought I had known what was going on. Café Mom's Away? People were now filling the living and dining rooms and coming precariously close to those antiques from other centuries. I began getting worried. "Nick," I said, "what are we going to do?"

He shrugged his shoulders. "I don't know." He looked dazed. Meanwhile, music blasted and kids were dancing in every room.

"Do you know what you've got here?" I asked him.

"A real mess." He glanced around the room.

"Café Mom's Away."

He seemed to have heard it before. "But who . . . ?" he asked, confused.

"Her," I said, pointing to the other side of the room.

He stormed over to Rochelle, who was devouring the entire bag of Fritos Louis the Ape had brought.

"What do you think you're doing?" he accosted her.

"Want some?" She held out the bag.

"Get off it!"

"Just thought we'd spend the shortest day of the year together." She glanced over to Louis the Ape, who was getting another drink. "Don't we always?" She batted her eyes coquettishly while glancing over to get my reaction.

"No, we don't," I heard him say.

"Come on, Nick." She smiled seductively. "It was only a joke. What happened to your sense of humor?"

"What happened to your brain?"

By now the sound level had risen hundreds of decibels, and you could hardly hear the person standing a foot away. People were dancing wildly between couches and credenzas, between the Ming and Sung dynasties, between the seventeenth and twentieth centuries.

"Nick. You better tell them to be careful." My concern was growing. Some of his photo friends and their dates were dancing too close to the porcelain vessels with long necks. One even wobbled and my heart dropped. Things were beginning to get out of hand. Louis the Ape was now gesturing wildly, doing some kind of sultan dance with Rochelle. Then he picked up the statue of the young boy with the flying carp.

"Got a catch," he said and laughed heartily. He seemed like such a brute to be holding something so delicate and fine. My heart stopped until he returned the piece to its rightful place. Miranda was dancing more sedately with Alex, the kettledrum boy. But they were about the only ones. The music was so loud the room shook, and the dancing had reached a frantic pitch. Hands were flying in the air, bodies gyrating to the beat.

"We'd better stop this," Nick said, as he ran to the stereo. But halfway there, we heard a tremendous crash. It sounded like hundreds of pieces of porcelain falling onto a wood-pegged floor. We stopped dead in our tracks.

Nick's expression turned to horror. The sound had come from the hallway. We ran in that direction. Pieces of onyx and jade were scattered everywhere. The dancing stopped.

In the center of the hallway floor lay shattered pieces of shimmering crystals, dials, and an hour hand. "Oh, no," I cried. "Not the chimera clock!" Nick couldn't say anything. He stood there speechless, staring at the pieces scattered around his feet.

Nellie was distraught. "I'm sorry," she managed to get the words out. "I didn't mean to. . . . It was an accident . . . I was . . ."

Neither Nick nor I could respond. "Maybe I can replace it. Buy another one," she offered feebly.

"It's irreplaceable." The words rolled off my tongue.

"Here. Let me clean it up." Nellie bent down to pick up some pieces.

"No!" Nick said. "Don't touch it!" His eyes were burning, his anger simmering just beneath the surface. His expression changed. I thought he could almost hear his mother's voice ringing in his ear. "The party's over. Everyone out. Get out of here!" His hands were trembling.

People grabbed their coats from the bedroom. Lynn and Lauren and Miranda and the rest. The coats that weren't collected fast enough, Nick threw in front of the door. "Whose are these?" he asked angrily.

Rochelle moved forward and grabbed her purple mouton jacket from the floor, dusting it off. And as she did, Nick grabbed her by the collar. "Get out of my house."

But Louis the Ape rushed to Rochelle's side. "Or what?" he said.

"Or you'll get your teeth bent in." Nick stood up to him.

"Oh, yeah? Listen, I'd tear you in two, but I don't want to break any more antiques around here."

I ran up to Nick. "Ignore him, he's just an air brain."

"Come on, let's go," Rochelle said, taking Louis the Ape's hand and walking out the door.

Nellie had her coat on and was heading toward the door. "I'm sorry. Really," she said to Nick. "I didn't mean it." I could see she felt miserable. But so did Nick. A part of me wanted to say something and make it easier for Nellie, but the words got stuck in my throat.

After the others had left, Carolyn, Dillon, Nick, and I stood staring at the shambles of the apartment. Empty soda cans, half-empty bottles of wine, pretzels, Twinkies wrappers. And tiny marble pieces scattered across the finely polished floor. Carolyn began clearing away the empty cans and wrappers. With a broom that Dillon found in the kitchen, he began sweeping up the pieces of the broken clock, but I took the broom from him. I held the marbleized hour hand and some of the mechanical workings, and the onyx and jade pieces that had made up the monster, feeling the weight of them.

Nick watched. He was too numb to do anything. His eyes grew colder. "Go home." His voice was frighteningly devoid of feeling, and it scared me.

Dillon was now wiping down the table.

"No, let me do it," Nick insisted. "Please go, I'll do the rest."

"But I want to stay with you. For a while," I begged.

"Please. I want to be alone."

"All right." Slowly I put on my coat and we all said good-night. I lingered behind. I hated leaving him like this. After buttoning up, I reached for his hand. "I'll call you later." And I closed the door behind us.

I did try calling that night. Saturday and Sunday, too. There was no answer. I pulled out his tape.

I don't know how to help him . . . I'm really worried. I only hope she doesn't kill him when she comes home. After all, she did love that chimera clock. But doesn't she love her son more?

Sunday evening, on the eighth try, someone finally answered Nick's phone. "Hello?" the voice said.

"Mrs. Buckley!" I nearly fell off my bed. "I thought you were in Hong Kong."

"Who is this?"

"Adriana."

She cleared her throat. "I was called back suddenly," she said in a terse inflection. "It seems my son got out of control and wrecked this place over the weekend."

"It's not like it looks, Mrs. Buckley," I tried explaining. "You see, it wasn't his fault . . ."

But she cut me off. "You won't be seeing much of him for a while," she said. "And frankly, I'm very disappointed in you."

126

"But Mrs. Buckley . . ."

"By the way, you had better find yourself another collaborator for your newspaper column, because Nick won't be using his camera for a while. He's been grounded."

I didn't know what to say. "I'm sorry," I mumbled.

"So am I," she said coolly, "but he's got to learn that he has promises to keep."

"But Mrs. Buckley, it wasn't . . ."

But she cut me off again. "Good night, Adriana." And she hung up.

I crawled into my bed and curled up into a small ball, rocking back and forth. It was all my fault. If it hadn't been for me and Rochelle trying to get even, none of this would have happened. Some winter solstice this turned out to be. If you ask me, some days aren't short enough.

TWENTY

The Monday following Christmas vacation I ran to school. I hadn't seen Nick for more than two weeks. Every time I called his house, there was either no answer or his mother picked up. What surprised me most was that, in all that time, he never called me. I was frantic. Devastated. I found it almost too painful to believe that he didn't want to talk to me at a time like this. At school, he was nowhere to be found. Not in the photo lab. Not around the halls or in the cafeteria. I even tried waiting outside his science and math classes. By the end of the day, I knew something was dreadfully wrong. It wasn't just that he was grounded.

I ran home, needing to talk. A half hour later the keys jingled in the door. All I had to do was glance at Mom's face.

"What happened?" I asked, alarmed.

"A man pulled a knife at me. He wanted more onion soup and the whole carton of Wonder Bread. 'Only two packages to a customer,' I said to him. 'You know the rules.' He didn't like that."

"What'd you do?" My heart was in my mouth.

"I gave him the whole friggin' carton. I mean, if he likes bread with onion soup that much. . . ."

I put my arm around her. "Maybe Dad is right. It's too dangerous down there."

She patted me on the shoulder. "So is crossing the street." She tossed off her shoes. "I think I need a cup of coffee. I know . . . let's go to Zabar's for cappuccino and a piece of butter cream cake. Let's make believe the last week didn't count and the new year starts today."

"But the phone."

"Turn the answering machine on. A watched phone never rings."

It's a good thing I didn't wait around. There was only one message and that was from a case that had graduated. Richard called as soon as we had walked in and said they had a bad snowstorm in Providence. He was shoveling the car out from four feet of snow.

I paced around my room that night, then pulled out Nick's tape.

Why didn't Nick call? You'd think he'd need to talk to me during these hard times. Instead, he's closing me out. It's as if all we shared together didn't mean anything. This was the first year I didn't make a new year's resolution. Why bother? Nothing seems to work out as you want anyway.

By nine o'clock I couldn't take it any longer, so I picked up the phone. "Hello, Mrs. Buckley, is Nick there?"

"No, he's not home now."

"He doesn't want to talk to me, that's it, isn't it?"

"I'll tell him you called when I see him." She hung up abruptly.

I returned to my tape.

What's wrong? All I know is I've got to speak to him whether he wants to or not. I know I can help. We're a team, and a team member doesn't let the other down when it seems like you're losing. Nick must be fighting inner battles. I'm scared. I really am. What if things are never the same again?

Next morning I was wearing the Jefferson button upside down. "I think I need a friend," I said, putting my pack down on the floor. They all wanted to help. "I'm afraid something has happened to Nick. And it's all my fault."

Lauren, who was ready to rehearse her Ophelia mad scene that morning, said she'd help.

"No," I said. "You have rehearsal. They need you in there."

"You need me out here, too. You've got to find Nick. And if you believe in it strongly, you'll make it happen."

"Thanks, Lauren, that's good advice."

"It should be. That's what you told me. Remember?"

Miranda was already devising a plan of action. Being a mystery story addict, she took the Agatha Christie approach, and started collecting hard facts and evidence. "Remember what F-E-A-R is. It's false evidence appearing real." She wanted to know all the details of his activities, then said she'd go snooping around his homeroom. Ask some of his friends.

"Are you sure you want to do that?" I asked her. "Ask all those people?" A few months ago, she had found it hard simply saying hello.

"Yes, Adriana, we've got to be methodical. A person can't just disappear. Why don't you let us help?" she replied.

Jane put on her horn-rimmed glasses. She'd cover the boy's gym after basketball practice. Nick always liked throwing a few baskets.

Nellie tried to console me. "Don't worry, you're Adriana Earthlight, Student Shrink. You'll make it work."

If only it was that easy. Even Ellen came to the rescue. She tried to make me feel better. "Maybe Nick doesn't want to be found yet." She took my hand. "People have different ways of showing they care."

Carolyn and Dillon offered to work together and speak to some of the kids on the fourth floor, where Nick had his locker.

It wasn't until I got to class that I realized my backpack wasn't over my shoulder. My tapes! I felt totally disoriented, like I was losing my mind. I remembered having it near the music room. I dashed back toward the music room as fast as I could. No one was in the halls. My pack was where I had left it. Frantically I searched inside. Only Nick's tape was gone. I searched the entire bag, dropping it upside down, spilling the entire contents. But no tape. As I threw books, papers, and old pencils back in, I heard Rochelle's warning months before: "Tapes got Nixon into a lot of trouble, too."

Class after class, I simply went through the motions. Biology. History. English. It didn't much matter. I was killing myself for being so stupid. So absentminded. To leave Nick's tape around was asking for trouble. It was too private for anyone's ears, especially the wrong ones.

In the middle of French, I could have sworn Mrs. Buckley walked by. I flew out of class and ran down the hall but I didn't see her. Then I heard the stairwell door close. I ran down after her. "Mrs. Buckley," I called. She stopped and turned around. "What are you doing here?" I asked.

"I came to speak to Mr. Saultern. He's the photography instructor. Nick's with him."

"With Mr. Saultern?" My mouth dropped open.

"He said Nick wanted to stay with him for a few days, to get himself together. He asked if it was all right. I said it was if he could help. Nick seems to be overreacting to this whole thing. I don't quite know why . . ."

"I've been speaking to a lot of people, here at school. Finding out things," she went on. "A girl with red hair and, uh, unusual flowered pants . . ."

"Nellie."

"Yes. She said she thought he had a great sense of humor. Then a boy named Alex told me that Nick always did exactly what he wanted and didn't care what people thought. He admired that about him. One boy in the photo lab even showed me some of Nick's awards. And his new work on sneakers."

"New! You mean you didn't know about that?"

Her elegantly straight nose twitched slightly in the air. "Not really." I perceived a crack in her cool exterior. She bit her lip.

"Mrs. Buckley. I think he needs you."

"It's probably too late."

"Is it? Well, he needs someone. Someone who knows what time he comes home at night. Knows what kind of day he had. If he ate right. Knows what he wants to do all the time. Mrs. Buckley, he needs someone who cares." She didn't flinch at my candidness. She didn't say a word.

"Why is Mr. Saultern doing this for Nick?" she asked me.

"He's about the most important person in Nick's life," I explained. "Didn't you know that?"

"Nick keeps a lot to himself," she replied.

I continued. "Did you know that Nick's so talented he's been submitted for the International Photography Contest? People respect him."

She played nervously with a folded piece of paper. Slowly, she began to speak. "I found out something today," she said, deep in thought.

"What?" I asked.

A faint smile swept across her face, almost transcending words. "I found out that Nick is pretty terrific."

"I could have told you that, Mrs. Buckley."

She continued her train of thought. "He's turning into a very interesting young man," she said, "in spite of me." Her tone was bittersweet. "Maybe when you speak to him, you can tell him that." She tightened her silk scarf around her neck.

"I think you should tell him yourself."

TWENTY-ONE

My parents arrived in Mrs. Crumper's office at eight in the morning. My father had not been amused when Crumper had called the night before asking for the pleasure of their company.

No sooner were we all in her office than Crumper began waving Nick's tape in the air like it was laundry. "That's private property," I screamed, trying to grab it away.

"Hands off." She yanked it out of my reach. Nick's name was written in my handwriting across the top, and I could tell by the way Crumper glared at me that she had listened.

"Where'd you get that?"

"I have my ways."

"Rochelle, wasn't it?" She didn't answer, but her look confirmed my suspicions.

"See this? It's Nick Buckley." She waved him up in the air. "His mother was in to see the headmaster. She's upset. Very upset. He's Adriana's latest case."

Mom looked surprised. "No. He's not her case."

"Afraid so," Crumper continued. "And he's flipping out, right as we speak."

"He is not flipping out. He's finding himself. There's a difference," I clarified.

"Oh. And what about Ellen? Those pseudo birthday cards sent her into a tailspin. And we're still peeling baked ziti off the wall from Carolyn's party."

Dad covered his surprise. "How can we help?" he asked in his most legal tone.

"She even told one impressionable student that it was fine to take six months off in South America to be a carpenter."

"He wanted to know what the real world was like."

"So you picked South America," Crumper lashed back. She shook her head hopelessly. "Your daughter's incorrigible. I've tried. Lord knows I've tried. A nice kid like Nick, and she drove him crazy."

"That's a lie!"

"Oh, is it? Then maybe your parents should hear this." She held the tape out toward me like the Wicked Witch of the West.

Mom simply shook her head. "I don't think so. We don't open her mail either."

"A week's probation might teach her a lesson," Mrs. Crumper said.

"Isn't that a bit harsh?" Mom said. "After all, she really didn't mean any harm."

"The most dangerous kind." Crumper humphed.

That gave Dad a moment to think. "Why don't you let us take her in tow?" he said. At that precise moment, a funeral in space didn't seem like such a bad idea.

I knew my rights, but I chose to remain silent.

Mrs. Crumper agreed to turn me over to the tight grip of my parents.

"Can I have the tape back?" I extended my hand.

"I think I'll just hold on to it for the time being." She slipped it into her desk drawer.

That night at home, Dad was livid. "I'm not spending a fortune on your education for you to be doing this stuff." He lowered the boom. They made me promise to cut out all my cases. They might just as well have asked for my left arm—and I'm left-handed.

That night I couldn't sleep. Snatches of dreams. Precipices. Losing footing . . . stranded on a rocky mountain and no way down. I woke up in a cold sweat.

The next morning I dragged myself out of bed, threw some old, wrinkled jeans on, skipped breakfast, and headed for school. I slowed down as I left my building, but no plane came sailing down. No sweet word of forgiveness, no silly design with wings and no body, not even a superglider. Nothing fell except a few sprinkles of snow. Who needed those stupid airplanes anyway. It was a childish game and I was all grown up now.

This time when I arrived at school, I had no button on, even though I needed help desperately. I told my cases we'd have to give up he underground temporarily. They agreed sadly. Next I found Mr. Saultern. He was deeply absorbed in work when I walked in.

"How's Nick?" I asked, in a subdued voice.

He turned around, holding up a picture, with a gleam in his eye. "My portrait for this year," he announced proudly. "What do you think?"

It was of an old man holding a young boy on his lap, his grandson probably. The old man had the same determined stare. "Haunting, like all the others," I replied.

"About Nick?" I asked again, but he took his hammer and started banging a nail into the wall, then hung up the picture.

"Is it straight?" He adjusted one side.

"You're supposed to care about him and all you're doing is hanging that ridiculous picture of yours."

He continued. Tap. Tap. Tap.

"Oh, you're just a silly old man," I lashed out in frustration.

His stare frightened me. "Why don't you fall off the edge of the universe."

I was dumbfounded. "That's not very nice."

"It doesn't mean what you think," he explained. "Why don't you go the limit. With all you got. And don't hold back."

"I don't get you," I said suspiciously.

"Go to the edge. Have the guts to be who you are."

He rubbed the rubber cement off his hands and grabbed a piece of number twelve paper, then scribbled an address. "Here." He handed me the paper. "It's a couple of blocks from here."

I clutched the paper. "Thanks, Mr. Saultern. Thanks so much," I sang out of the lab.

English could wait. So could American history. But Nick couldn't, nor could I.

"Happy birthday," I called back. "I love your new picture. I love your whole family up there."

" 'Bye," I heard his voice trailing after me. "Just don't get any older than I am."

"I won't," I called back.

TWENTY-TWO

I dashed down the street toward Lexington Avenue, then picked up my pace heading downtown. Just one last assignment, I promised myself as I ran the few blocks. I moved as fast as I could, making the most of the lights. Joy and terror mingled at the thought of seeing him again. All I wanted to do was run into his arms and tell him how much I cared. There was so much to say that words danced in my head at incredible speed. I knew I loved him but I'd never realized how much until this moment. I was ready to get closer to the edge. Ready to fall off. Nothing could stop me now.

Mr. Saultern's apartment was in an old brownstone, a little run-down. Fortunately, a neighbor arrived with his grocery bag so I slipped in right behind and ran up the stairs. I rang 4C. My heart was pounding. After a moment, I knocked. Faint music played inside. I was sure I heard someone sitting in a chair. No answer. I knocked harder this time.

"Who's there?" Nick answered suspiciously.

"Nick, it's me!" I gulped. Then silence. No response. "No one's with me. It's safe." My ear was flat against the door. "Let me in."

After a few turns of the lock, the door swung open and I rushed into Nick's arms. "I was so worried about you. We didn't know what happened." It poured out. "All I kept thinking about was you. If you were all right. If you needed anything. If I could help." His arms were limp around me, little tension in his shoulders. Actually, the greatest tension, at that moment, was between us. It frightened me and I pulled away. He had heavy circles under his eyes. "You're not sleeping. Nick, are you all right?"

"Great. Just great," he answered sarcastically.

"That was stupid of me. I'm sorry."

He walked back into the apartment and I followed. The apartment was small, cozy, and simple, exactly the kind you'd expect Mr. Saultern to have. Cluttered corners. Stacks of papers. Books everywhere. A few soft pillows on the couch were the only feminine touch. They must have been picked out by his wife years ago.

"Nick, I saw your mother Tuesday. She's very worried."

"Will you butt out!"

"Don't you think she cares about you?"

"I have no parents." He turned his back to me and looked at his watch.

"Your fifty minutes are over." Nick walked toward the door.

"Why are you pushing me away? Pushing away people who care about you?"

"Like my father?"

"You never really talk about him, but he's always on your mind, isn't he?"

"That's none of your business."

"But there must be things you want to know. Deserve to know."

"I swear you've got a disease."

I paused. "I have a great idea. Maybe your camera and my tape recorder should go out instead," I said flippantly.

He pointed me toward the door. "Fine," he replied. "My Nikon will give your Sony a call." Then he opened the door to show me out.

"It's not me you're really angry with, is it?"

"Cut the crap, Dr. Adriana Earthlight, I'm finished with your analyzing."

"It's a piece of your childhood. A piece that's missing. A piece you'll need before you can grow up."

"I said I was finished," he replied coldly, trying to close me out.

My mind jumped to my mother's birthday, my age next year, my father's lucky number, and Richard's soccer shirt. "Yes. And I think I know what it is."

"Oh, yeah?

"What are you so afraid of?" I asked.

"What are you so afraid of?" he repeated.

"What are you? A parrot?"

"Boy. You're good at asking questions."

"And what is that supposed to mean?"

"Have you ever wondered why you're so busy asking other people the very questions you should be asking yourself?"

I was taken aback. "No, I haven't."

"Well, you really should," he continued. "You live everyone else's life but your own. It's safer."

"You're just getting back at me for what I said, aren't you?"

"See what I mean? More questions. What do you think of this? That? How does it make you feel?" He stared directly at me as I stood there with my mouth open. "Adriana," he continued, "you're too busy with everyone else's problems. When will you start looking at your own?"

I wanted to run as far away from this room as possible. "Is that what you've been doing here all this time? Thinking about what's wrong with me?" I asked angrily.

"See? Another question." He shook his head. "Isn't it time to get on with your own life?"

"Isn't it time to get on with yours?"

With that, he reached over and grabbed my shoulders. "Do I have to shake you? Stop it," he said, holding my shoulders tightly. "Who else is going to tell you except someone who cares about you? Most people wouldn't take the time. Adriana. Wake up!"

I stared at him. "I need my cases."

"I think you need them more than they need you."

"That's a lie!" I screamed.

We both stood there in silence. "Everything seems to be coming out all wrong," I said, shaking my head sadly. "I better go."

"One more thing, all that talk about trust. All that talk about us being special. All I was was another case, wasn't I?"

"What do you mean?"

"You were the first person I ever let get close to me." He covered his eyes with his hands.

"Nick." I moved closer but he recoiled.

"That's why it hurts. Because I trusted you," he said.

"How did I let you down? What are you talking about?" I asked.

He searched under a pile of magazines. "I'm talking about this!" He pulled out the missing tape and held it up in his hand.

I tried acting innocent, but my world was falling apart. "Where'd you get that?" I feebly asked, my body shaking. "Rochelle, wasn't it? She made copies!"

"What'd you file me under? Lunatic? Fool?"

I stumbled around at a loss for words. "Nick, I never . . . meant . . . to . . . hurt you. I just . . . ."

"Just couldn't help it. Made me case number sixteen and just forgot to tell me. So I'm the last to know."

"No, it wasn't like that at all. You're my boyfriend, not . . ."

"Sounds like semantics to me. You're good at that, Adriana."

"But, Nick, I love you."

"You've got some way of showing it. You don't know when to stop."

"Maybe I don't." Tears welled up in my eyes and I didn't want him to see my cry. Not this time. Instead, I grabbed my backpack and turned to leave. I started down the hall, but he called after me.

"Adriana, on second thought, you take it." He handed me the tape. "Use the flip side. Cross my name out and write yours."

I grabbed the tape and ran to the stairs. Our team was finished.

TWENTY-THREE

I arrived home without any memory of getting there.

Familiar smells. Leather. Wood. Lemon Pledge. Smells of home. I threw my jacket on the chair. Nothing mattered. The house was empty and I felt terribly alone. I sank into the living room couch and cried. All seemed lost. Then I felt a hand touch my shoulder.

"Richard! I didn't know you were home."

He sat there and let me cry, even handed me a tissue. After a while, he began to talk. "What's wrong?"

"Everything. Nick was lost and then I found him. Crumper got hold of the tapes and so did Nick. And that rotten Rochelle did it. And now he hates me. Everything's fallen apart."

"Wait a minute. You're losing me."

"See, the parts got all mixed up. Cases. Boyfriends. I didn't mean to make a tape of him, but I couldn't help myself. It was like a . . . a . . . compulsion."

He sat there and listened to me.

"And that's not all," I said.

"More?" he asked incredulously.

"Nick said I was using my cases to run away from myself. Oh, Richard, it's true. You said so yourself. I'm a fake. A phony."

"You are not. You've got a gift."

"Ha! Some gift." I rolled the tissue into tiny balls. "I'm the thickest of all. At least the others are trying. . . . Look at me.

Hiding behind them. How do you feel about this? About that? Oh, Richard, I'm just one big fat failure."

"Hey, wait a minute," he said. "Stop badmouthing my sister."

"Please, Richard," I begged, "I need the truth."

"The truth." He pondered that a moment.

I blew my nose, waiting for more advice.

"Have you got those tapes in your closet?"

I nodded.

"Why don't you see what questions you asked the others? Ask yourself the same ones."

That was a thought.

"And, Adriana, you're always on the phone."

"Now you're telling me to yank my phone out?"

"Just turn it off after business hours. And take time to do a few things you enjoy, like painting."

"But you always tell me I'm awful."

"Who cares what I say? Paint your little heart out."

I got up and threw my arms around him. "As far as brothers go, you're not so bad." Then I headed to my room.

"Where are you going?"

"You're absolutely right. But I'm not giving up on Nick."

Richard bolted up in his chair. "I thought we were talking about you."

"We were, but I've got to help him before it's too late."

In my room, I opened a can of diet soda and a bag of cookies. I wandered around nervously, this way and that, eating cookies, biting my nails, rummaging through a few drawers. The bottom of my closet began to bother me. The fallen sweaters and wrinkled shirts, mismatched shoes. Stuffed animals that had fallen down on my head. I looked at myself in the mirror.

That's when I felt a strange sensation, a little kernel inside my chest, a flutter.

It was almost not there, but I placed my hand over the spot. Nothing moved, yet everything moved. A tear rolled down my face. I was thinking, really thinking, about myself—for the first time. I wanted to memorize the sensation. I sat there for a long time, then reached for the phone.

"Hello, Mrs. Buckley. I saw Nick. He seems . . . well . . . troubled."

"Does he want to see me?"

"Not yet. He doesn't want to see me either."

"Oh, Adriana. Who's left?"

Who *is* left? I thought to myself as I hung up. I washed my face and ran a brush through my hair, then passed Richard's room on the way out. "Say, do you remember the number on your soccer shirt?"

"Who remembers that?"

"Please. It's a matter of life and death."

"Sounds serious."

"It is. Think about it." I headed for the door. "I need a little air."

I wandered around the city. The park. The boat basin. Strawberry Fields. Imagine. No destination. That's why I was surprised to find myself in front of Mr. Saultern's building looking up to the fourth floor. A light was on. Nick had to be up there. If only he would stare down at that exact moment and rush down to me.

But the window was empty. No faces appeared magically. No one rushed down. I started home. The city was turning to shadows. It was almost dark.

When I walked in the door, Richard had something behind his back. "Look what I found." He waved the soccer shirt in the air.

"Number eighteen." I jumped in the air.

The next day at school, I had a breakdown. I ran down to
peek in the lab. Nick wasn't there, just an intermediate photography class. The smell of developer brought back memories
of the darkroom. Those silly feet, the amber safelight. Our
first kiss. The contest. Mom's and my feet making the finals.
The photo of that woman stared down at me and wouldn't let
go. Her staring past the farm, past her property, past her life,
had an inner strength. She had courage. Courage to change
the things she could, and the strength to leave what she
couldn't.

I gulped and ran down the hall.

I knew what I had to do and prayed that it wouldn't be too
late.

TWENTY-FOUR

I ran to my room and closed the door behind me. The area code was easy, 201 for New Jersey. Then I carefully dialed my mother's birthday, my age, almost, Dad's lucky number, and Richard's soccer shirt. My nerves were running away with me. To my horror, someone answered.

"Hello," the voice said.

I was about to hang up. Words got stuck in my throat. "Hello," I managed to get out. "Is this Mr. Buckley? Trevor Buckley?" My voice wavered slightly on his first name.

"Yes . . ." He sounded hesitant.

"Do you have a minute?" I asked him.

"Well, I was just getting ready to leave for a conference. Who's this?"

"Adriana," I replied.

"Do I know you?"

"No . . . ," I answered, "but you're Nick's father, aren't you?" This man sounded like he was in a rush, off somewhere like Nick's mother, off on his own business. Nick just didn't seem to be anybody's business.

"Is there something wrong?" He paused. "Is he sick?"

"Not exactly. Not in the hospital sense, or anything like that."

"That's good." He sighed, sounding relieved.

Why does someone have to be in physical pain to warrant immediate attention? "But I think he's given up," I went on.

There was silence at the other end. "On himself," I explained further.

"Well, how can I help?" he asked me.

"That's just the point. I think only you can. Please." I heard his hesitation, so I pressed harder. "Can't you try?"

An interminable silence. "You wouldn't understand," he said.

"Maybe I would."

"What'd you say your name was?"

"Adriana. My friends call me Adriana Earthlight."

"Earthlight, hey?" He laughed nicely. "Does Nick know you're calling?"

"He'd kill me if he found out."

"I thought so."

"See, he'd never call you himself."

"Don't I know that."

"But that doesn't mean he doesn't want to speak to you."

"Isn't his mother there?"

"I don't think his mother can help him right now. I think it's you he needs."

He paused. "I'll tell you what. I have to be in the city on Monday. For a meeting. Let's say I'll meet him before that."

"That's wonderful, Mr. Buckley. I thank you. Nick thanks you."

"I wouldn't be so sure about that. Listen. Tell Nick I'll meet him at the apartment at seven-thirty in the morning."

"Oh, no, he's not there," I replied. "But I'll take you to him."

"Where is he?" For the first time he sounded concerned.

"At Mr. Saultern's. See, he's left home. Temporarily."

"Who is this Mr. Saultern?" he questioned me suspiciously.

"A teacher from school. And about the only person Nick

will trust right now." My throat choked at the admission.

He paused. "All right. Meet you there at seven-thirty."

"I'll wait, even if I have to cut French, bio, and . . ."

"No, you won't have to do that," he assured me. "But how will I know you?"

"I have dark hair and I'll be wearing a tweed coat and purple scarf."

"I'll be in a safari jacket. Things might get a lot warmer when I get there. I'll be expecting anything."

"Good-bye." I started to hang up.

"Wait a minute. Where's the apartment?"

"How could I have forgotten? Corner of Lexington and Seventy-fifth. The east side." Then I hung up. Aren't phones wonderful. The plan was moving ahead.

TWENTY-FIVE

I had recurring nightmares that my alarm wouldn't go off and Mr. Buckley would leave. Every hour I'd wake and check the time. Finally, it was six-thirty. I dressed in a hurry and skipped breakfast. Mom grew suspicious as she watched me frantically searching for my purple scarf.

"Wear the red one," Mom suggested, slipping it around my neck.

"No! I want the purple one!"

"My, you're touchy this morning."

"No, I'm not," I snapped as I found the purple scarf and twirled it around my neck.

To my surprise, a paper glider sailed down to my feet. The fleet was flying again!

The most natural beauty is honesty, and don't cut corners.

Incredible. A witch mother. If a part of her knew my secret, she didn't utter a word to me.

By seven-fifteen, I stood waiting on the corner of Seventy-fifth and Lexington.

I had never gone so far off the deep end. But there was no turning back.

Seven—forty-five, fifteen minutes late, but who can expect accuracy during morning rush-hour traffic. A car was parked across the street. A man with straight dark hair, wearing a tawny brown suede jacket, got out and headed toward me, and I knew immediately it was Mr. Buckley. I lit up. The plan was working. This was beyond talk, beyond my wildest expectations. This was my greatest case yet! His eyes caught mine as I pointed to my purple scarf.

He was taller than I had expected, over six feet, and, on closer inspection, graying around the temples. Nick had his bone structure and the same look around the eyes. Mostly, I thought, he seemed kinder than I had expected from Nick's ogre description, and somewhat older than in the picture on Nick's shelf. But, of course, that was taken over six years ago, on another continent. Another world.

"Are you the mystery voice?" he asked.

"Yes. Are you the mystery father?"

"So it seems." He nodded. "My son has good taste."

"Thank you. But I'm a few inches too short," I answered nervously. I always found it hard accepting compliments graciously.

I pressed Mr. Saultern's buzzer and prayed silently. "I didn't tell him you were coming. But when he sees you—"

"Don't expect miracles," he cut me off. "I don't think he likes me very much right now."

"I don't think he likes anyone very much right now."

No one answered. I pressed the buzzer again, worriedly this time.

"Remember, we're in this together," he said. I felt an instant camaraderie.

"Yes?" Mr. Saultern finally responded in a morning tone.

"It's me, Adriana. Nick there?"

"He went off to school this morning."

"Oh," I answered, surprised. "Thanks. I'll see him there."

Mr. Buckley didn't seem thrown by the slight change of plans.

We entered the school building. It was in the usual Jefferson morning frenzy. Not a word passed between us as I led him downstairs. Mr. Buckley appeared lost in his own thoughts.

The photo lab was still. Not a trace of life. Then I panicked. What if these two ships passed each other for another six years? Mr. Buckley poked around somewhat apprehensively.

"I'll see if he's heading for his first class," I suggested.

Mr. Buckley's eyes kept darting around the room. Images seemed to be bouncing off the wall at him. Then his eyes fell on a few photos in the corner.

"Nick's," I said, pointing to the Adidases and Mary Janes. "And those are my feet." I covered my mouth, half-embarrassed.

"You're photogenic," he teased. We both laughed and it broke the tension for a moment.

"I'll be right back."

Halfway down the hall I saw Nick heading for the lab. Quickly I ducked out of sight behind the stairwell. No camera hung around his neck and the usual bounce was gone. He seemed sadder, as if his spirit was gone. He walked unsuspectingly into the lab.

At last they were in the same room together, the first time in six years, sharing the same space, and yet they were light-years apart.

I listened. Silence. I moved a little closer to the door to hear better.

"Dad!" Nick finally said. He was caught off guard.

"Hello, son," Mr. Buckley spoke awkwardly.

Another pause, then a few more words. "What are you doing here?" Those were the first words Nick had said to his father in six years. "Don't tell me you were in the neighborhood. Or is it Parents' Day?" His voice was angry and cold.

"You look well. Taller."

"I got tired of being four-foot-eight. Grown seventeen inches since I last saw you. That happens, you know."

"You were always tall for your age, Nicholas."

"No one calls me that anymore."

"Nicky, then," he corrected himself. "Nick. You're making it harder. Please."

"Please what? Please don't mind the letters that never came. Or the birthday cards. Please what? Please leave you alone?"

"You're angry with me, understandably."

"Damn right I am!"

"I didn't think you wanted to hear from me."

"Oh, is that it? Dad, didn't you ever want to be with me? All those years? Even once? Didn't you wonder how the kid's doing?" His voice trailed off. "What am I, a hunk of junk?" Nick sounded really angry now. "Oh, so what," he added. "I don't need a father anymore."

Just then Rochelle, with her jet black hair twisted in some fancy roll, bounced into view, heading directly for ground zero.

I intercepted her.

"Out of my way, Shortie." She pushed me aside.

"Not on your life," I said, giving the orders now. She tried shoving me aside, but no way was I going to let her pass. I was ready for combat. Nothing was going to ruin what was turning into a fiasco on its own. Rochelle grabbed my wrist, but I remembered some old judo tricks Richard had taught me, and with a sudden jerk, she landed on the floor, surprised.

"You're a poor excuse for a person," I said. "You're selfish and mean. All you think about is what's in it for you."

She jumped to her feet, about to lunge.

"Just try it," I said in my judo stance, "and your angora will be pressed fur."

Slowly and precisely she straightened her sweater. "Fortunately for you, I have a sociology test," she said.

As she left I heard footsteps coming in my direction. I darted around a corner, unseen, and watched Nick and his father walk down the corridor.

Boy, I really blew it! How did it fall apart so soon? They didn't even give themselves a chance. Less than ten minutes. It had such potential. I really messed things up royally. I kept admonishing myself—why can't I leave things alone? Eight–thirty-five and half of history class was over. Mr. Wexler had been covering Andrew Jackson and the Age of Revolt, but who needed a classroom when you could play war right in the basement of Jefferson High.

TWENTY-SIX

Having to give up my underground cases left me with plenty of time for myself and for feeling lost and alone. I longed for the mornings the way they used to be. The March issue of *The Centurion* came out without "Footnotes." Lots of kids asked where the article was.

I began spending more and more time alone. Lying around my room. Taking long walks. Even trying to write a poem or two. So much was building inside me that I didn't understand. All I knew was that everything I'd thought important in my life was gone. The tape recorder remained in my top desk drawer untouched for weeks, and I tried searching for something else to hang on to.

Almost three months had passed since the fiasco between Nick and his father. I wished I could blot it out. Nick never connected me with the incident and I never told him. Since we weren't talking, it hardly mattered anymore. Nick and I had virtually become strangers. Hard to believe the closeness we had shared not too long ago was over. But I couldn't get him out of my mind, no matter how hard I tried.

Carolyn and I were waiting for spring. It was late and we could always tell the moment it arrived, regardless of the calendar. Winter seemed to drag on forever this year.

On April fifteenth, income tax day, Lauren found me moping out of French class.

"What is it?" I asked. I could tell she had news.

"My father told the magazine he wasn't going to move until I finished the school year. That it was too hard on me. And you know what they said?"

"What?"

"That he could wait until July. Moving was hard enough. They didn't want an unhappy family."

"That's wonderful," I cried.

She absentmindly crunched an old sheet of looseleaf paper into a ball.

"Why are you crunching that paper like you're packing?" I asked her.

She twisted her hands into a pretzel, surprised. "Habit." We both laughed, before she picked up on my mood.

"You miss Nick, don't you?" she asked.

"A lot."

"You told me once that a part of a person is with you no matter how far away you go."

"Oh, Lauren. I'm going to miss you." And we hugged each other tightly.

"I'm not leaving yet. *Hamlet* opens in two months. You better be there."

"Nothing can keep me away."

"To be or not to be," Lauren said." I guess we're all trying to answer that one."

"Sure are." I replied. "We sure are."

I saw that as a turning point. That evening Miranda called. Alex had asked her to work on a duet of "Satin Doll," then have dinner.

"What'd you say?"

"Yes. I said yes!" she cried happily. "And guess what? He's been wanting to ask me out for a long time."

"I guess he found his own way."

———

The last month or so of school always involved incredible studying. Wexler's term paper was due, and we had a long-term biology assignment to build on a functioning aspect of the human anatomy. I didn't pick the heart since mine had mechanical failure. Instead, I found myself building a globe of the human brain, pinpointing the hypothalamus and centers of thought, reasoning, and emotion. I thought of it as similar to a globe of the world, where I could actually put my finger on previously unseen and untouchable territories.

A week went by. Miranda was off to the movies for her second date with Alex. Jane had a few enouraging conversations with Roger, the chess boy, who actually offered to teach her some strategy of the game. It was her move and she made one. Even Ellen seemed happier.

My cases were getting better. They didn't need my therapy anymore. I found myself taking out the old paint box and an unused canvas. The tubes were clogged so I dug holes with a screw driver. Deep cobalt blue and aquamarine began oozing out again. Pinks and violets. Cadmium yellow. Hours passed while I painted. I forgot all about my troubles.

Whem Mom returned with the groceries I ran to show her the finished canvas. She studied it from different angles. "Very nice," she said approvingly. I helped her unpack the groceries, then took a can of mothballs she had bought and tossed a handful along the top shelf of my closet, around the old shoe boxes with tapes. My hands ran along the cardboard rims. I missed my tape recorder. I missed my dictating. I was trying to kick the habit, but I didn't know it would be so difficult.

Then it happened. Wednesday afternoon Mr. Wexler threw open the third-floor window. Spring came in! Carolyn and I did the only thing we could: cut class and spend the rest of the day out of doors.

The day was balmy and warm, the kind you dream about during those long, cold wintry days. Others suffered from spring fever, too. The park was full of people, all with jackets flung over their shoulders. Then we saw our first daffodil of the season and we knew our instincts had been right.

"Tomorrow's Dillon's and my first anniversary," Carolyn told me as we stopped to look at some cherry blossoms about to open. "We made it through one whole year."

We laughed and I thought about Nick. "Relationships are sure hard work," I said.

We walked past the boathouse, vaguely looking for the snail wondering if he survived the winter, too. "Don't you wish it could have stayed simple forever? No problems. No worries."

"Oh, I don't mind." She rolled up her sleeves. "You know, Dillon can say whatever he wants and it doesn't drive me crazy anymore. And I just say whatever I want back. It sure is a lot more fun. And I think he likes me better for it. I'm free. Free."

With spring officially ushered in, my spirits improved dramatically. The world didn't seem such a dark, lonely place. I suddenly began to see new possibilities. As sad as it made me, I even began to see life without Nick.

TWENTY-SEVEN

Only once, in a weak moment, did I pick up the phone and dial Nick's number. But I hung up after the first ring.

One Saturday night Mom and Dad had tickets for Circle in the Square Repertory Theatre, and Richard had a date with a new girl from Long Island. That meant the apartment would be mine for a few hours. There was nothing like self-imposed silence, and I was beginning to enjoy being alone.

I wandered around each room aimlessly, not quite knowing what to do with myself. The kitchen towels needed refolding and the hydrangea appeared slightly on the dry side. I puffed pillows and straightened the crooked calendar over my desk. Then I passed my closet. I opened the door. Hours of activities had always existed inside before. Sadly my eyes glanced up at that familiar shelf where all my shoe boxes overflowed with hundreds of secret wants and private pains. How neat those boxes remained, hundreds of tapes collected, organized month by month, each person with his own shoe box. Carolyn was in a boot box—she had the biggest, being my first case and my oldest friend. A small, square blue one was in the corner. It was in that box that I had started to put Nick. There they stood. All in a row. They didn't need my anymore. My cases seemed better, and if not totally cured, certainly on the right track.

At my dresser I played with a small, hand-carved box my father had brought back from a business trip to Munich. The inlaid wood was supposedly cut from the Black Forest, formed into rosettes; when the top opened, the box played "Edelweiss."

I listened to the tune for a few seconds. As I did, a strange sensation happened, a tightening in my chest—or was it a mass of weight where it had previously been weightless? I closed my eyes and tried to listen. It was still small, almost imperceptible, but maybe in a few months or years that voice would grow louder and clearer, full and strong enough so it could tell me the secrets of my body and my mind.

I bolted back to the closet door. I stared up at those boxes and realized at that moment that my happiness was in a large part a commitment to other people; but I could bring happiness to others only by being happy myself. It was my time to stand at the edge of the universe. I climbed on the desk chair and pulled down the small blue stationery box. I darted over to the desk with Nick's tape in my hand, and, with a large black marker, I crossed off his name and wrote my own.

Then I walked into the kitchen and turned the answering machine on, flipped the Record dial to the left, and began speaking, slowly at first, but clearly. "You have reached Adriana Earthlight. Sorry I am not at home to answer your call right now, but I am out on the most important case of all."

TWENTY-EIGHT

Hamlet had Lauren working around the clock, between homework and long rehearsal hours in the theater. Ms. Greene, the director, required two hundred percent of her, but Lauren had never been happier. She had come to life in a way I had never seen before. The first performance was Friday, three days away, and she was searching for an electric curling iron to give her hair tight ringlets for her mad scene. I pulled mine out from the back of the bathroom cabinet. I didn't need tight ringlets anymore.

The worst part of my madness for Nick seemed over. The agonizing part. Now all I had to do was learn to love someone else.

I grabbed the tape recorder and began dictating.

Here it is almost the end of school, many months since Nick and I broke up. Seems like a lifetime. I still miss him so much. I miss what we had together. He made me feel beautiful. Alive. But unlike Ophelia, Nick won't drive me over the brink. Loving Nick has made me stronger. Sharing my fears, secrets, and dreams with him has changed me. It must have been even harder for Nick to trust me than it was for me to trust him. And I let him down. I never would have believed that my half of our collaboration would be the weakest link. If only Nick and I had met when we were both a little older. A little smarter. Perhaps we would have had a better chance . . . but no going back. There is something I have learned. That is how fulfilling it is to love . . . how wonderful it is sharing your life with another person. And I thank him for giving me that.

The next afternoon I was putting the finishing touches on my globe of the human brain. The hypothalamus was painted a dark green and I had just finished pinpointing the spot which the physiology book indicated was the center of emotion. After a second coat, I set the globe to dry.

The intercom buzzed as I was washing off the paint.

"Somebody here to see you," the new doorman announced hesitantly. "Didn't get the name."

"Be right down," I replied. Probably Carolyn on her way home from the diet center. She'd lost fifteen pounds and wanted to celebrate. Or Miranda.

Key in hand, I dashed downstairs.

The doorman pointed to someone waiting near the mail-room. A middle-aged woman hugging a Yorkshire terrier under her arm was leafing through her mail. Then, behind her, I saw Nick. His camera was slung around his neck and he was photographing a Chinese delivery boy from the Hot Wok. I pinched myself to make certain Nick was actually standing in my lobby. His deep, penetrating blue eyes held me captive as always. That intriguing, magnetic gaze. And seeing him again stirred all those raw emotions I'd felt the first day, all those feelings I had buried for months. He smiled as he saw me approaching.

"Hi," he said.

"Hi." I smiled back nervously.

"Long time, huh?"

"Yeah." I shook my head. "So you're shooting the entire delivery boy now."

"Thinking of going into fuller shots. Maybe even color." He seemed in motion against a row of hi-tech mailboxes as he fiddled with a circular he'd picked up.

"Well, that *is* a change," I replied.

"I tried calling you lots of times."

"I never got the message."

"That's 'cause I hung up."

"I did the same," I confessed.

"You know, I could kill you for what you did. Calling my father."

I gulped and looked away. "I know, it wasn't any of my business."

"No, it wasn't."

"I'm sorry. I had no right to interfere."

"Can you believe he didn't write or come to see me because he thought it would be better for me?"

"How could he think that?"

"Mom told him that after each visit I'd act up. Cause trouble at school. Seem real unhappy. That he was hurting me by seeing me. As if that could hurt me! All the other kids had fathers," he continued. "All I wanted was him. I'd even have settled for a visit once a year."

"Would you?"

"Anything would have been better than nothing. Imagine. He said Mom fought for sole custody. That he wasn't a stable influence. He got visitation rights only two weeks out of the year."

"Why didn't he use them then?"

"Good question. He said he was on the other side of the world. Now he's only across the Hudson."

"That can still be halfway around the world if someone wants it to be."

"Yeah. He finally admitted he was selfish. That he was doing what was best for him, not for me."

"He admitted that?"

Nick nodded. "Then he asked how he could make it up to

me. Make up all those lost years!"

"How can anyone make that up?"

"Exactly. That's what I asked him. Then he said he was afraid he'd lost his son."

"Has he?"

"I don't know. I mean he can't start reading me bedtime stories or tucking me in."

"Maybe there can be other things."

"Maybe."

The mailroom was quiet, and I could hear Nick swallow. His eyes were full of tears and I knew by looking at him that everything was possible.

"Can you forgive me for calling your father?" I looked searchingly into his eyes.

"Forgive you!" he said, surprised. "I could kiss you for what you did."

"Really?"

"Yes. I'm very happy you can't stop yourself."

I turned away slightly. "I've given up my cases."

"I don't believe it. Why?"

"You always told me I was meddling."

"I didn't mean it. Besides, I didn't expect you to listen."

"Well, it seemed that if this would-be shrink didn't change direction she could cause some real trouble."

"But you have a gift. A talent. You can't just throw it away. It's rare to have a passion like yours. You inspire me."

"Come on," I replied, not believing him.

"Really." He moved closer to me and touched my face gently. "You know, I couldn't get you out of my mind. Even when I was mad at you I kept thinking about you. Your determination. Spirit. How pretty you are."

I was unable to move a muscle.

"I have never felt this way before, Adriana, and I don't

know what you did. No one has affected me like you have. But I had to straighten myself out before I could tell you that. I have something for you," he said, slowly bringing his hand around to the front.

"A bird of paradise!"

"Like it?" He watched my response.

"Like it! You know I do." I touched the orange petals with some embarrassment. "You knew all the time I sent it, didn't you?"

"Uhhhuh."

"Why didn't you say anything?"

"Flowers say it all. Isn't nature wonderful!"

"Do you think so?" I touched the flaming orange bursts. My words had sounded abrupt.

"What is it?" He picked up on my change in tone.

"Nick." I searched carefully for the right words. "I want you to be the first person to know who I am, really am. The good and the bad. But the problem is, I have to know first."

He played with his camera nervously, trying to understand what I was trying to say.

"It seems so rare to get a second chance. And here we are. I don't want to lose you," I said, suddenly worried. Nick looked so vulnerable standing there against the mailboxes. "Will you wait for me a little bit?" I asked him.

"You know I will," he answered without a moment's hesitation. "Maybe I can help."

"There are times when I feel no one can help. Not even you. See, I need you so badly it scares me. Do you understand?"

He took my hand in his. "I think so."

"Funny"—I looked up at him—"I never thought I'd like being alone. In that way, I'm getting to be a little like you."

"And maybe I'm getting to be a little like you. A little more outgoing." He pushed a strand of hair off my face. The moment grew too intense.

"It's nice to see the camera around your neck again," I said, breaking the mood. "Can I see it?"

He removed the camera and I focused the lens and took a picture of him.

"I bet you'd be good at photography." Then he changed the subject. "I forgot to tell you."

"What?"

"The photo contest. Portrait of an American Sole."

"Yes . . . ?"

"Well, I won!"

"You didn't!" I said, jumping out and down. People in the lobby turned.

"Ssssh," he quieted me.

"Why didn't you tell me before? Then you'll be leaving. For the safari. July?"

He paused. "My father invited me to join him in Canada this summer. He's doing some work there. It's really beautiful, he says. Great fishing, especially near Nova Scotia. They have giant salmon."

"Like they sell in Zabar's?"

"Except these are the ones that got away."

"What are you going to do? Give up the contest?"

The glint in his eyes told me he'd already made up his mind.

"Heck, no! I worked too hard for that contest. I'm not giving it up."

"But what about your father?"

"I'll see him at the end of the summer. We'll have the month of August. After all, we'll have our whole lives."

I smiled.

A bleeping electronic sound came from Nick's wrist. He glanced down. "Five-fifty and twenty seconds. My mother's waiting. I said I'd be at home at six. She holds me to it."

"So, you're speaking again?"

"I moved back."

"I'm glad."

"I stopped by the lake on the way here."

"Our snail?" I guessed.

"Let's look for him together. Maybe we can stop there on the way to *Hamlet*. Want to go with me Friday night?"

"To go or not to go is not the question." I took liberty with Shakespeare's famous quotation. "To want to go is. And I'd love to."

"Great. Let's have dinner first. The Boathouse Café. Pick you up at five-thirty."

He nodded good-bye and began to walk away, but our eyes never left each other. We gazed achingly until we couldn't bear it anymore and then we ran into each other's arms. We held each other so tightly we could hardly breathe. Nick was right. The best conversations were without words. Almost without breath!

When we pulled apart, he held my hand and lingered. "I better go," he said. "God, you look so beautiful now."

Yes, I thought, words were nice, too, as I watched Nick turn the corner and walk back into my life.

TWENTY-NINE

After taking our next-to-last final, Carolyn and I darted around the corner to the coffee shop for the biggest chocolate ice-cream soda they could make. Our brains had been over-stretched.

Some of the other girls had beaten us there and we pulled a table over to them. Carolyn went on about being separated from Dillon for eight weeks while she went on a cross-country student tour and Dillon stayed in the city working with his band. Miranda planned on leaving in a few weeks to be a counselor-in-training at a camp for the performing arts. Lauren just sat listening to the plans. She didn't say much. We all knew her plans and none of us wanted to deal with it. Nellie said she was going to try her hand at modeling and voice-overs for commercials; an agency had already expressed interest in sending her out. And Jane confessed she planned a summer in therapy with Dr. Milton Goldfinger. This time she was going to start a self-improvement program from the inside out.

"Did you hear Rochelle's plans?" Carolyn asked. "She's going with her family to Paris and study French at all the local designer boutiques along Rue Saint-Honoré." We laughed.

"What are you doing to do?" Miranda asked me.

I blew chocolate bubbles around the bottom of the glass. "I don't know yet," I admitted.

"Don't wait too long," Nellie said. "We only have two and

a half months before we'll be back at school as seniors."

Carolyn nearly dropped her straw. "Please! Don't rush it."

We paid the check and returned to class. On my way to biology a familiar voice called my name.

"Can you please come in for a moment?" The Crumper beckoned, wiggling her finger. I complied.

The Crumper bent over the aquarium. "Housecleaning," she explained. "So you made it through another year?"

"You seem surprised."

"You've got to admit, it was touch and go." Her mood had become decidedly more relaxed, a less critical edge in her voice.

"I suppose." I smiled.

She continued her chores. "Well, kid, I wanted you to know that I'm taking that long-awaited subbatical. But I'm not exactly going to be doing nothing. Just taking a year off from this place. Go to the movies. Maybe take ballet. And in between do a little research."

"I'm glad, Mrs. Crumper. It seemed that's what you really wanted."

"You know," she went on, "you remind me a lot of myself when I was your age. I was more like you than you'd like to believe. Young. Filled with idealism, passion, hope. I think that's what rubs me the wrong way about you. That's why I'm harder on you than on the other kids."

"Why?" I asked her.

"I don't want you to fall. If I can get you angry enough, you'll fight for what you want with everything you've got, kid."

"Mrs. Crumper," I said. "When you don't ask for help and you really need it, that's when you're really in trouble. Don't you believe that? And that it's healthy to search for something better?"

"Yes, Adriana. Absolutely. I tell my groups that. When all goes well we never bother to look. Ah, but when we're really depressed"—her eyes lit up—"and miserable, that can be a place to grow from."

I stood there, startled. She was human, after all.

"Listen, you." She came toward me. "I'm taking a year off from this place and when I get back, if you're lucky and I'm lucky, you won't be here. You'll be in college."

We both laughed.

When I reached the door, I turned back. "Mrs. Crumper?"

"Yes?"

"Thank you for being hard on me."

"Don't mention it, kid. It was my pleasure."

The last period Friday was study hall, which I cut, since there wasn't much to study for. The last exam on Monday was English and it was an essay on Steinbeck's *The Pearl*. All my energy was devoted to the *Hamlet* opening and my date with Nick.

Before leaving I popped my head into the theater to wish Lauren luck. Ms. Greene was just about to begin the second run-through. Nerves were taut, so I just gave Lauren a hug and left her a Mars bar for a predinner supplement.

The clock in the school lobby said two-fifteen. Only three hours before Nick would arrive, and there was lots to do. Carolyn and I ran for the crosstown bus, then she caught her second bus, and I walked the five blocks home.

I washed my hair and blew it dry. Then twisted those floppy, bendable curlers around strands of hair. If only I had practiced setting it more. The pearlized pink nail polish camouflaged these two nails I had bitten off during the French exam. They would hardly show. But it was hard to polish my nails, because my hands were shaking. I tried to keep my hand steady long enough to put green liner on my eyelids. Nick was due in only forty-five minutes. Some blush, pink lipstick. Pulled the rollers out and shook my head back and forth to make the curls bounce back. Daring. Different. Thank goodness Mom had ironed my white dress. I yanked it off the hanger and the zipper got caught only once as I slipped into it. I'd worn it only once before, to an afternoon wedding, and it still smelled new. There. The preparations were complete. I stared at myself in the mirror, taking a good, hard look. And I liked what I saw. For the first time in months, I felt really pretty.

The buzzer rang. Nick. I ran for the door.

Nick stood there, surprised. "Wow!" His eyes lit up. "You look great."

"So do you." I had never seen him in a suit and tie before, and there was something elegant about his appearance and the way he carried himself. I couldn't believe he was actually here to take me out.

In the elevator, Nick adjusted his tie. "I couldn't wait for tonight," he admitted.

"Me, too," I responded.

He continued staring at me. "I've never seen you look this pretty. I like your hair."

"Thank you. It took all afternoon."

"So did picking out this tie. Think it goes?"

"Definitely," I answered, not knowing a thing about ties.

He started sniffing around my neck.

"You're tickling me," I giggled, loving his touch.

"What's that?"

"Obsession," I imitated the low, sexy voice in the television commercial.

"I like it." The elevator door opened in the lobby and we

caught a glance of ourselves leaving. We made a great couple.

We entered the park at Central Park West and Eighty-first Street, and I picked up speed.

"What's the rush?" he asked.

I didn't want to tell him the rush was in my head. At the end of my fingertips. In every cell. When we arrived at the lake, there were no telltale signs of familiar snail life.

"Be careful. You'll get dirty. "Nick picked a piece of dirt off my dress.

"That's okay. Our snail's worth the smudges."

The ground was soft under our feet from last night's rain, and lush enough to support crawling colonies of all kinds.

"Over here," Nick called near a clump of shrubbery. The undergrowth of tangled leaves concealed a whole cluster of snails with little ones. "I think that one's ours," he said, pointing to a shell with circular lines winding around the middle: his fingerprint. If it wasn't our snail himself, it was his new family.

The Boat House Café shone in the distance. The maître d' gave us a preferred table along the lake's edge, and we ate dinner watching the sun slipping down toward the towering trees. The city was shimmering in the early evening light.

A sleek black gondola docked a few yards away. It appeared surreal against the backdrop of the skyline of Central Park South and midtown Manhattan. When we finished the chocolate chip pie and paid the check, Nick pushed back his chair. "Be right back," he said, and returned minutes later waving two tickets. "Señorita." He extended his arm. I slipped mine through his, and he led me onto the black boat. The gondolier at the stern made lazy patterns in the water with his single oar.

" 'And silent rows the songless,' " Nick quoted. "Byron."

His arm slipped around my shoulders and I nestled closer, resting my head on his chest. The slow sound of the oar lapping the water transported us to our own Venetian canal. No one else existed. No one. And then the sun had set and it was time to go. . . .

When we arrived at Jefferson, most of the good seats were taken, but Carolyn called from across the theater.

"Over here," she said, signaling. "I've saved you seats." Dillon was having a few good laughs with Allen, sitting next to him, and Nellie was laughing along. Miranda, too. Jane was in a row behind, surprisingly underplayed, even wearing her glasses. The chess boy sat next to her. Only Ellen seemed alone. Or so I thought, until she turned and talked to Paul.

Ellen held flowers on her lap, the opening night present we had all chipped in to buy for Lauren.

All my former cases were there. But now they were just good friends. I looked at them sitting across the rows and realized how they had helped me, too.

Nick and I walked to our seats. Jerri and Terry whispered and laughed, obviously dissecting us. Rochelle, right behind them, was in incredibly glamorous linen with the latest leather accessories. Some things never change.

The lights began to dim and a hush fell over the theater. The show was about to begin and I suddenly got chills.

The crimson curtain started to rise on a large, stone castle in Denmark. Soldiers stood there on the alert. Then I felt Nick's arm edging along the blue velvet seat. I reached until our hands found each other in the dark, and then our fingers intertwined tightly. My special hour had come.